THE GRANDPA KILLER

A LUCA MYSTERY
BOOK 10

DAN PETROSINI

Copyright © 2023 The Grandpa Killer by Dan Petrosini.

All rights reserved.

No part of this publication may be reproduced, distributed, or transmitted in any form or by any means, including photocopying, recording, or other electronic or mechanical methods, without the prior written permission of the publisher, except in the case of brief quotations embodied in critical reviews and certain other noncommercial uses permitted by copyright law. For permission requests, contact dan@danpetrosini.com

Print ISBN: 978-1-960286-10-9
Naples, FL
Library of Congress Control Number: 2023901538

ACKNOWLEDGMENTS

Special thanks to Julie, Stephanie and Jennifer for their love and support, and thanks to Squad Sergeant Craig Perrilli for his counsel on the real world of law enforcement. He helps me keep it real.

OTHER BOOKS BY DAN

THE LUCA MYSTERY SERIES

Am I the Killer

Vanished

The Serenity Murder

Third Chances

A Cold, Hard Case

Cop or Killer?

Silencing Salter

A Killer Missteps

Uncertain Stakes

The Grandpa Killer

Dangerous Revenge

Where Are They

Buried at the Lake

The Preserve Killer

No One is Safe

SUSPENSEFUL SECRETS

Cory's Dilemma

Cory's Flight

Cory's Shift

OTHER WORKS BY DAN PETROSINI

The Final Enemy

Complicit Witness

Push Back

Ambition Cliff

1

———

IT SHOULDN'T SEEM A SURPRISE WHEN SOMEONE IN THEIR eighties meets their maker, but when a string of otherwise healthy octogenarians made that meeting sooner than expected, I got an itchy feeling that somebody had a thing against grandpas.

———

IT WAS one of those perfect spring evenings, with plenty of daylight to spare. The lakes were high, the humidity low, and everything was as green as it could get.

The combination was one of the things I loved most about Southwest Florida, but instead of reveling in it, I was unsettled.

I knew what Dr. Bilotti said about being present was true, especially with your kids, or you'd miss half of life. But here I was, playing Trouble with my daughter but feeling like a sinkhole was about to open.

"Daddy, it's your turn."

I pressed the plastic bubble. "Here comes a six."

Mary Ann opened the slider and stumbled coming out.

"You all right?"

"Yeah."

"Maybe you should stop wearing flip-flops."

"Come here."

"I'll be right back, Jessie."

Mary Ann whispered, "Ronnie's father, Bill Coby, died."

"What? Bill was in great shape."

"I feel so bad for him."

"When I helped Ronnie move him into Palm Shores, he carried more stuff than me."

"I figured he'd live till a hundred."

"Poor guy just bought that place. It's massive; you should see it."

"They said he liked it, that there was a lot to do there."

"The funeral's Wednesday. They're going to do just one day."

"Good. I remember as a kid sitting in a room with the casket for three days. And nobody said a word back then. It was creepy."

I GOT BACK to the house after dropping off the babysitter. Mary Ann was tiptoeing out of Jessie's room with a finger to her lips. I followed her into the bedroom. She said, "I thought she was going to get up when she heard the garage door."

Taking my tie off, I said, "Ronnie took losing his father harder than I expected."

"They were close. He had him around a long time."

"Ronnie said they're going to lose ninety grand on the apartment."

"What do you mean?"

"His father paid over three hundred thousand for the place, and they're only going to get back two and a quarter."

"Why is that?"

"His dad paid a higher price to get lower monthly fees, but he didn't live long enough for it to make sense."

"But he was only there for a couple of months."

"I know, but according to him, that's the way it works with a lot of these places."

"That's stupid."

"I'm sure there's more to it than that."

"Maybe. You know, Maria said someone called Ronnie and told him their father died at Palm Shores a month ago. He was supposedly in phenomenal shape, and they think something funny is going on."

"A conspiracy to kill old people?"

"That's what she said."

"How old was this other guy?"

"I think eighty-one."

"Still above average."

"Not for Naples."

She was right. The lifespan for people living in Naples was about eighty-four, one of the highest in the country.

I DREAMT Jessie was in her fifties. She looked like an older version of Mary Ann. She was cutting up the food on the plate in front of me. She stabbed a string bean and was telling me to open my mouth, when my cell phone rang.

It was just after three in the morning. It was the sheriff, and he rarely called unless there was a body. I scooted into the closet.

"What's going on, sir?"

"Looks like the burglary ring struck again, in the Moorings. Only this time, the homeowners were sleeping when they broke in."

We had a team of thieves that were hitting vacation getaways or homes only used during the winter season. The gang would storm a house, disable the alarm system, and be out in minutes. It was a serious crime ring, but nobody had been hurt—yet. Sheriff Chester's brother-in-law was the president of the Naples Real Estate Association. That relationship, and the fact we hadn't had a homicide in eight months, prompted the sheriff to have us drop a cold case and focus on the bandits.

"It might not be them if it's a home invasion."

"The homeowner flew in with his wife earlier tonight."

"And the thieves thought the home was empty. Anybody hurt?"

"Unfortunately, they pistol-whipped them."

Ouch. "I don't like that; they're armed."

"I know. It could have been worse."

"Where are the victims?"

"NCH Baker. Joe and Clara Williams. I'd like you to get what you can from them."

"I'll be there before seven, sir."

"We have to shut this ring down, and fast. The housing market is slowing down already."

Was there really a need to remind him that real estate always slowed down as the days in May fell away? "We'll do what we can, as fast as possible."

"Keep me in the loop."

"I will, sir."

"Sorry to get you out of bed."

"That's okay, sir. Good night."

It wasn't all right to wake us up in the middle of the night.

It was a serious crime, but there was nothing we could do until the morning.

Walking into the bedroom, Mary Ann said, "What's the matter?"

"Another home break-in. The homeowners were sleeping when it happened."

"Scary."

"Go back to sleep."

Before I could adjust my pillow, I could tell by her breathing that Mary Ann was already out. It would take me a good hour to get to sleep with the thoughts romping around in my head.

If it turned out that it was the same gang who had beaten the homeowners tonight, it meant their intelligence gathering wasn't sophisticated. Maybe it was nothing more than a landscaper tipping off the ring that a home was empty.

The gang was getting more brazen by the month. When Chester asked me to take over the investigation, the thieves had ramped up their activity from one home a month to two. It was troubling, but it could lead them to a mistake.

Assaulting homeowners was an aggressive escalation that didn't fit. Why not restrain them, take what you wanted, and leave? The couple had been sleeping and were stunned to find someone in the house. It was unnecessary violence, and though reckless behavior led to arrests, it also led to people getting killed.

2

Sipping my coffee as the sky began to brighten, I called the station and had the break-in report emailed to me. I read through it, letting the java work its magic. I took another gulp and made a call to NCH's Baker Hospital.

The news was good; the couple had been released after being treated. They weren't seriously injured, just shaken up. As expected, they were up when I called.

Over a bowl of Cheerios, I looked over the report. It was six thirty, and my girls were still asleep when I headed to the Moorings to interview the couple.

The Moorings was a community with a big reputation and price tags to go with it. It had its own feel and was close to the Gulf of Mexico. They even had a private beach to use, which was valuable during high season. Riding through the center of the area, I admired the homes on either side of Crayton Road.

Just past the Moorings Golf Club I turned onto Putter Point Drive. The home where the crime had occurred was sitting at the end of the cul-de-sac. Backing up to a golf course, the off-white home was the size of a boutique hotel.

The landscape lights were on as I pulled onto a circular driveway anchored by a tiered fountain.

Getting out of the Cherokee, I checked the fountain for algae. It was clean. Fountains needed regular maintenance or they'd grow hair. Someone was looking out for this palace while the king and queen were away.

My thoughts shifted to what these people did for a living. Surveying the outside of the mini-castle, Joe Williams swung open the Mediterranean home's ten-foot door.

Light streamed onto the driveway. "Good morning, Detective."

"Morning, Mr. Williams." The sixty-two-year-old had a three-inch square of gauze taped to his right cheek. The area was red but would turn purple before the sun set.

"Come on in. Clara just put a pot of coffee on."

The foyer and main room were covered in a checkerboard pattern of black and white marble. All the lights were on. The interior had a contemporary feel. My eyes gravitated to the empty spaces on three walls. A museum light was shining on a blank wall.

This was some home. I could understand why thieves would target this place.

"Do you have a security system?"

He frowned. "Yes, but we don't use it. I don't know why. Up North, we always alarm the house."

He seemed like an everyday guy, not someone who lived in a home of grandeur. Was he really grounded, or had the robbery knocked him off his horse?

We stepped into a kitchen with two islands. "This is my wife, Clara. This is Detective Luca."

"Good morning, ma'am."

She had a nasty bruise on her neck just below the jawline. "How do you like your coffee?"

"Just a splash of milk, please."

We sat around a kitchen table with a floral centerpiece. It seemed too fancy for coffee.

"Last night must have been frightening."

Clara's chin began quivering, and Joe reached for her hand, saying, "It was, but we thank God we weren't seriously hurt."

"Tell me what happened."

"Clara went to bed around ten thirty. I sat on the lanai reading for about forty-five minutes before turning in. Something woke me up; it was one forty. It was a cracking sound. Then I heard voices. I woke Clara up and told her someone was in the house. I went to lock the master door, but this man burst in and cracked me right here." He pointed to his cheek. "Clara started screaming, and he told her to shut up and he— he hit her."

"Did you see what he looked like?"

"He had a black ski mask on. He pointed the gun at us and said to hand over our phones. Then he made us get in the bathroom, telling us not to turn the lights on."

"What about his build?"

"He was big. I'm five ten, so he was about six foot but broad."

"Any limp? Tattoo?"

"He was wearing a black, long-sleeved sweatshirt with a hood."

"Did you see anyone else?"

"No, but there were two other voices. One had a Spanish accent; the other, I'm not sure what it was, maybe East European or something like that."

"The statement you gave last night listed what was stolen. Was there anything else?"

"Not that we can tell."

"The paintings that were stolen. What can you tell me about them?"

"We're not collectors, but we enjoy art. We like the contemporary stuff, not too far out though."

"Were they by well-known artists?"

"Not really, more like up and coming."

"Expensive?"

He shook his head. "Just a couple of thousand each."

That was expensive to me, but it wouldn't bring more than a couple of hundred from a fence.

"Did you buy them from the same dealer?"

"No. We hunt around, and if we find something, we'll get it if we really like it."

"Got it. How often do you use the home?"

"As often as we can. Clara retired from teaching, and I'm doing my best to slow down."

"What do you do for living?"

"I have a landscape company in Maryland."

Must be a large enterprise. "How long was it since your last visit?"

"About four weeks ago, right, honey?"

"Yes, we left right after Easter."

"You came in last night?"

"Yes, we arrived about nine o'clock."

"Did you tell anyone you were coming in?"

"No, I mean, just a few friends, to get together with."

Joe said, "And the club, I called for a tee time this morning. Oh geez, remind me to cancel that."

"Do you use a home watch service?"

"Yes, AAA Home Services. They're supposed to come once a week."

"I'm going to need a list of any service companies that would know you were not around. Not that you notified, like the home watch people, but anyone who comes around and can tell the home is empty. Landscapers, pest control, your fountain service, the pool company, things like that."

Clara's eyes widened. "You think it was someone we use, that we pay?"

"We don't know. At this point, we believe someone is feeding information that the homes are empty. If we can identify a pattern, it could lead to catching these thieves."

Clara grabbed a pad off the counter and began writing.

3

AFTER THE FUNERAL MASS AND INTERMENT, THE FAMILY HELD a repass luncheon at Brio's. It was a long day, but the process undoubtedly helped dent the grief. Bill was just about to turn eighty-five. His death shouldn't have been a surprise, but everyone there, including Mary Ann and me, were stunned.

Considering his physical shape and energy level, most people thought he'd be around for a decade longer.

I didn't know about another ten years, putting him at ninety-five. It was possible, but like a baby, there was a world of difference in an octogenarian with each passing year.

It was always tough being the first to leave an event like this, but the story about the new crime had gotten around. It provided cover and I left. Mary Ann would hitch a ride with a neighbor.

DERRICK WAS STANDING in front of a map that marked the location of the burglaries. A handful of pins was concentrated in the area between Livingston Road and the gulf to the west, and Golden Gate Boulevard and Pine Ridge to the north.

"How was the funeral?"

"It was sad; he was an amazing guy. You should have seen him. The guy went to the gym every day."

"You can't live forever, but at least he had a good quality of life."

"He did. It took him a while when his wife died, but he bounced back. Even just moved into Palm Shores."

"Where's that?"

"A little past Tin City, kind of behind that Naples Grande place."

"Oh, I know where. How did it go with the Williamses?"

"You should see that house. I bet it goes for two, maybe even three million."

"What's he do?"

"The wife's a retired teacher. He owns a landscaping business, but unless he does government work, he probably inherited the money."

"How bad were their injuries?"

"They got lucky. He got whacked on the cheek, and she got it on the neck. I don't know if the thug was being nice, but she's lucky he didn't hit her face."

"It's the same gang, right?"

"Probably. They could have surprised them, or they're getting ballsy."

"I cross-checked service companies. There's a couple of overlaps but no pattern."

"We have to focus on the stolen goods. It's mostly electronics and paintings. Who's going to buy the paintings? They paid a couple of grand each, but what are they going to get for them on the street?"

"Every home had pictures taken off the walls."

"Cross-check the places where they bought them. See if there's a common thread."

"I'll get on it. Hey, you missed the action before."

"What action?"

"Guess who was here?"

I had been up since five. The last thing I wanted was to play a guessing game. "You really got to stop it with this guessing stuff."

"Sorry. A whole group of people came in, some kind of advocacy group for people in nursing homes. They wanted to meet with the sheriff. They say there's abuse and deaths from neglect."

"I saw something on the news about a week ago where some woman was suing Lake View Care because her mother had fallen and broken her hip. Poor woman never recovered and died. The daughter claimed Lake View was negligent because they knew she was at risk to fall. I felt bad hearing about it, but these places can't control everything."

"I saw this post on Facebook where this guy's dad got one of those viruses that are resistant to antibiotics in a place in Atlanta. This guy said his father and two others died from it. He sued, and they settled because the place didn't put the person who got it first into quarantine."

"What are they going to do with all of the baby boomers when they need care?"

"We're going to go broke. I'm not for it, but maybe this euthanasia thing, you know, maybe there's a way to find some middle ground."

"I get it for those in pain, for sure. Terminal illnesses that cause tremendous suffering. There's no way anyone should have to go through that. That said, it's a slippery slope. Other people deciding on what is a good quality of life for someone else is dangerous."

"I couldn't pull the plug on someone."

"Me either. Unless someone was in a coma and brain dead, I wouldn't be able to take them off life support. I'd be haunted by it."

READING *Cat in the Hat* to Jessie put us both to sleep. It wasn't the story; it was the lack of sleep. At least for me. Mary Ann took Jessie from my lap and put her to bed. I took a sip of water. When Mary Ann came back in, I put the TV on.

She grabbed the remote, lowering the volume. "She's restless."

Looking for something to watch, I began cycling through channels.

"Put the news on. I want to see the weather for tomorrow. We're going to Clam Pass."

I wanted to tell her to check her phone. It was at least as accurate as the fifteen minutes of nonsense the news spent on the weather. "How can you go without me?"

"Take the day off."

"You know we have to give a week's notice."

"Look, it's Chester."

The sheriff was talking to a reporter. It concerned the demands that he look into the nursing home deaths and the reports of abuse.

"Derrick said a group came to the station today. I'm surprised they didn't go to the press."

Chester told the reporter he was going to appoint a task force to look into the allegations. Task force was a reassuring phrase, but it could mean one detective. I thought it was a good idea, as long as I wasn't involved.

4
——————

Derrick brought a folder over. "Frank, it's not every burglary, but take a look at this."

It was a list of the burglaries and the names of the places where each victim had bought their artwork. He'd drawn a red circle around a name that provided more than half of the stolen pictures.

"Um, interesting, but I don't know what this commonality means. It could be these are the go-to places if you want something nicer than what Wilson has, but you don't want to get crazy with a zillion-dollar painting from Sotheby's."

"I'm going to take a ride down to the art district by J and C Boulevard and stop in a couple of these places. You never know."

I didn't believe it would advance the case, but as he said, you never know. "Go for it."

"You mind if I take off after that? Lynn has a doctor's appointment. They're concerned about her blood pressure and sugar levels."

"No problem. Don't be too concerned about it. Many women, Mary Ann included, get diabetes and high blood pressure when they're pregnant. It usually goes away after they give birth."

"That's what the doctor said. I'm not worried, just want to be there for her."

"Take as much time as you need. Let me know how it goes."

When Derrick left, I began cross-checking the landscapers who took care of the burgled homes. It was easy to suspect a worker of selling info to supplement their pay, but the chances of the same crew working on each home were slim. Just over half the homes used WLM, but they were a large company in the space.

The dispatcher for WLM told me that there were four different teams that maintained the houses in question. It didn't seem to be them. I grabbed the list of pool companies. You couldn't drive a mile without seeing a vehicle from a pool service or air-conditioning outfit.

I don't know how the pool maintenance companies made any money. We paid eighty dollars a month. They came once a week, and the fee included all the chemicals. They knew when someone was away and would skip a week when it happened.

My cell rang. It was my neighbor Ronnie.

"Hey, Ronnie. How are you guys doing?"

"We're okay. Half the time I still think Pop is around."

"It's tough. I'm sorry. If we can help, let us know."

"Thanks. Look, I don't want to sound like a lunatic, but I just couldn't let it pass."

"What's going on?"

"It could be nothing, but I got a call from this guy, John Martin. His father also lived in Palm Shores. He passed away about a month before my dad did. Anyway, he tells me his father was the picture of health, and he died suddenly, just like my pop."

"What was the cause of his death?"

"They told him it was natural."

"And he thinks otherwise?"

"Yeah, he thinks something is going on at Palm Shores. He even said that there was a woman who died the month before, and she was only seventy-nine."

Only? "You want me to check around a little?"

"I know you're busy, but if you could, I'd appreciate it. I owe it to Dad. If anything is going on, it's got to be stopped, and I know it's not related, but I saw the news about Lake View last night."

He was right; it was unrelated. "Let me have Mr. Martin's contact info."

THE HOME on Longboat Drive stuck out. It was new and fashionable. The coastal contemporary style was accelerating, and it was one change I approved of. The houses on either side were at least thirty years old. If their owners weren't old-timers, they might be shamed into knocking their homes down or doing a major remodel.

A squad car blocked the home's driveway. In the front and in the rear of the home was water that was part of the Gordon River system and led to the Gulf of Mexico. The thieves had targeted another home in an expensive neighborhood.

In this case, the burglary probably happened a day before anyone realized. A neighbor saw an open rear slider. The woman knew the owners were away and called 911.

No matter what direction you turned, there were water views. The place had wide plank flooring throughout the entire home. I liked it but wasn't sure how it would hold up with a six-year-old dropping juices every other day. My eyes zoomed in on a glass wine closet that was tucked under a staircase. It wasn't big, but it was sweet.

Opening the door to see how cold it was, I got a blast of sixty-degree air. Half of the shelving was empty. Was the owner a wine lover, or was this a designer's idea?

I counted three empty picture hooks. It appeared a table lamp was missing along with a sizable TV. The kitchen looked to be intact. I stepped onto the lanai. An infinity pool appeared to flow into the Gordon River. To the left, a forty-foot boat was raised above the water.

After discounting the use of a boat, I headed in and checked upstairs. The master had a deck that would capture amazing sunsets, though I doubted anyone traipsed up to see them.

The master closet had been ransacked. It was impossible to assess without the owner's input. Two other bedrooms seemed untouched, and I went back to the main level.

Forensics would dust for fingerprints, but this gang had always worn gloves. I didn't think anything would come of it. The owners were flying in from Denver. I'd speak with them after they assessed the loss.

Thankfully, no one had been hurt, but if it was the same gang, it was the second time their MO had changed. First, they'd broken in when someone was home, injuring them. Now, they had dramatically sped up the time before striking. The Longboat home had been hit right after the Moorings one.

5

THE OWNERS OF THE LONGBOAT DRIVE HOME, SALLY AND Robert Crenshaw, were in their early fifties. Flying time from Denver to Fort Myers was four and a half hours. The Crenshaws were so fresh, I wondered if they took a private jet.

"As I mentioned, we believe the same group is responsible. We're following several leads."

The husband nodded shakily, but I caught the wife rolling her eyes. They were understandably traumatized by the burglary, but she looked like someone who would complain that a pool was at eighty-five degrees, not eighty-six.

"Who knew the home was going to be vacant?"

She said, "It's not like we broadcasted that we were leaving."

"Who was aware you were not home? Landscapers? Pest control?"

He said, "The Klines, they're our next-door neighbors. We always tell them in case they see something, and they did. But other than that, we're both very busy in Denver and keep to ourselves while we're here."

"He doesn't even like to go out to dinner much."

"Is there anything missing that had a high value?"

She said, "Our artwork is the only thing we care about."

"That's not true, Sally."

I said, "There were six pieces stolen. Is that correct?"

"Yes."

"Any of them more valuable than the rest?"

"Yes—"

The husband cut her off. "Caroline was particularly fond of a piece that reminds her of the place we met, but it didn't cost any more than the others."

"Do you have a list of the pieces and where they were bought?"

He looked at his wife and said, "Uh, I think we do somewhere. I'll have to look around for it."

"That would be helpful. I'd like a list of anyone who services the home for you. Pool company, landscaper, that sort of thing."

They conferred for a moment and jotted down a list of names. I thanked them, telling them I'd be in touch as the case developed.

On the way out, I scanned where the artwork had been hung. Heavy-duty hooks marked each location, but there was just one museum light hanging over an empty spot.

BACK IN THE OFFICE, I noticed the yellow Post-it with John Martin's telephone number on it. I didn't want to call him, but I had told Ronnie I would, and when I gave my word, it meant something.

A pet peeve of mine was people saying they were going to do this or that but never did. Most of the time it was harmless, but it reflected on the person and their reputation.

Instead of declaring you're going to do something that you probably won't, just add a qualifier and you're off the hook.

"John Martin?"

"Yes, who is this?"

"Detective Luca with the Collier Sheriff's Office."

"You're Ronnie's neighbor, right?"

"Yes. He asked me to speak with you about your concerns regarding Palm Shores."

"They're more than concerns. Something is going on there. Healthy people, like my dad and Ronnie's, are dying just a couple of months after moving in there."

"That is troubling, but I'd imagine there's quite an adjustment moving into a facility like that."

"Facility? It's a country club for seniors, is what it is. My dad was happy there until they killed him."

"What leads you to believe his death wasn't natural?"

"Dad was in perfect health. He played tennis three days a week, for God's sake. Then, all of a sudden, they say he passed during the night? You know, when it happened, we were stunned, but I just thought something inside him gave out. But then I get a call from this woman, Yolanda. Her mother died a couple of weeks before my father. She tells me her mother died a month after she went on Medicaid. She said she knows of at least two other cases like that."

"I don't understand the Medicaid reference. How is that relevant?"

"It's all about the money. You see, Palm Shores wants you to pay out of your pocket; they call it private pay. When you run out of money, they can't just kick you out. You go on Medicaid, but Medicaid pays like half what a private payer does."

The financial gain to be had by eliminating residents the state paid for was an interesting angle. However, it implied a large conspiracy. Whoever owned the place would benefit, but they'd need a death squad to carry out the executions.

"I understand your concern about the reimbursement rate, but killing someone over a couple of thousand dollars a month would be a stretch."

"Yeah? First off, it's more like five thousand a month, but what about the money they get to keep for guys like my dad and Ronnie's father? They take a huge haircut when they die."

I recalled what Ronnie said: his dad opted for lower monthly fees, paying over three hundred thousand for an apartment that could only be sold back to Palm Shores for twenty-five percent less. Considering his health, it seemed like a good bet as he'd save two thousand a month. He needed to live three years to break even but died just two months later.

"I'll look into this. Give me Yolanda's contact information. I'd like to speak to her as well."

After hanging up, I leaned back in my chair. This sounded crazy. The place where you'd go to be taken care of would kill you? Though I understood the financial gain side of such a scheme, it seemed incredibly difficult and dangerous to pull off.

Losing a loved one was emotional, and we needed someone to blame for the pain we felt. In this case, it appeared the bogeyman was a faceless institution.

I didn't want to talk to this Yolanda, but if Chester pulled me into the nursing home investigation, I might learn something about Medicaid from her.

"Yolanda Sykes?"

"That's me."

"Detective Luca from the sheriff's office. Mr. Martin said I should speak to you."

"I can't believe it. Somebody's finally waking up."

"Tell me what you believe happened to your mother."

"Palm Shores killed her because she couldn't pay anymore."

"And how did they do that?"

"I don't know. They just did and said she died naturally."

"You could have requested an autopsy if you felt there was something suspicious about it."

"I wanted to, but my brothers didn't want to have my mom go through that."

"I understand. Do you have any evidence foul play was involved?"

"Look, not even a month after she goes on Medicaid, she's dead. And she's not the only one."

"It could have been a coincidence."

"No way. You know, some lady who works there warned me to get my mother out since she was going on Medicaid."

"Did she provide specifics as to why?"

"No, she said she couldn't talk; she needed the job."

If the employee said anything, she could have been referring to the quality of care or even the food. "An accusation that your mother was murdered by Palm Shores because of her inability to pay is a serious charge. In order for the sheriff's office to investigate, we're going to need more than what you've told me. Is there something concrete I can work with?"

She gave me the name of the woman who worked at Palm Shores and pleaded with me to speak with her. To display concern for her allegations, I asked her to forward the death certificate to me and to ask her mother's doctors for her health records.

6

———————

It was another one of those bright mornings that enhanced the belief it was good to be alive. I told myself it was going to be a good day as I walked into my office.

There was a manila envelope sitting in the center of my desk. It was marked "Personal and Confidential" in black magic marker. The sender was Yolanda Sykes. I hesitated before picking it up, wondering if my mood was going to slide.

It contained the death certificate for her mother, Rosa Sykes, and a file from her doctor. I examined the death document. The cause of death was listed as acute cardiac syndrome. A quick Google of the term confirmed my guess; it was heart related.

Norman Krieger, MD, had certified the death of Rosa Sykes, who was seventy-nine. The doctor's address was the same as the place of death. Dr. Krieger seemed to be employed by Palm Shores.

A box near the bottom was checked. It meant the death wasn't reported to the medical examiner and was consistent with the notation that an autopsy hadn't been performed.

Rosa Sykes' medical records were numerous and confusing. She was taking a small dose of Zocor to control her cholesterol, and one other medication, levothyroxine. Google revealed it was for her thyroid.

According to a chart of visits, she hadn't had a physical in fifteen months. Maybe the doctor at Palm Shores had administered one. Her blood pressure was one hundred thirty over eighty-five. A solid reading.

Stuffing the paperwork into another envelope, an inter-county one, I addressed it to Dr. Bilotti. Let him review the records to see if there were any warning signs that could explain a heart attack.

***

THE SHERIFF PEERED over his reading glasses. "Take a seat, Frank."

"Thank you, sir."

"What's with this patrol request?"

"We're working a couple of angles regarding the stolen goods, but by having cars out in their target areas, we could get lucky."

"Luck? Is that what we're relying on?"

"No, but it's an effective deterrent, and we might catch them in the act."

"You're asking for almost every unmarked car the force has."

"We're covering an area from Livingston to the water and between Pine Ridge and Golden Gate."

"Do you realize the overtime this would demand?"

"Sorry, sir."

He tossed his readers on the desk. "We don't have the extra money for something like this. The lab is sucking resources like a ten-year-old drinks soda. I moved funds around in the last budget, but I have nowhere to pull resources from."

"I'll take a look at reducing the patrols and cutting surveillance hours to reduce the OT."

"You know I'm a cop, not a bean counter. I never liked the budgeting aspect of this job. I get pressure when a crime happens and pressure when I ask for the money we need to protect the citizens of this county."

He was half right. Chester wasn't a cop or an accountant; he was a politician. The way I saw it, he needed to glad-hand his way with the county commissioners for the necessary funds. It was his problem.

I shrugged, and he said, "And Commissioner White wants me to form a task force to look into nursing homes. What about the money we're going to need for something like that?"

"I saw you on TV talking about looking into it."

"I had to. What else could I say? That it should be handled by the state? Tell them to get the Elder Affairs Division involved? That wouldn't go over well. I'm telling you, it's a zero-sum game."

"On the positive side, I don't believe this gang knew the homeowners of the Moorings place were home. Maybe they lashed out when they found them home."

"They're targeting high-end homes."

Of course, they were going where the money was. "But with the owners out of town, there's no jewels or cash laying around."

"The real estate community is getting nervous over what it could do to the marketplace. The high end goes, it'll take everything with it."

Chester was another one who focused on the big homes in

Naples. There was money in this town, but there were a thousand coach homes for every mansion. Many middle-class people called Naples home. Maybe the high-end boutiques and a couple of overpriced restaurants would close, but we'd be fine if this got a bit worse.

"There's nothing for them to worry about. What's puzzling is the risk they're taking versus what they're stealing. I don't care if the TVs are the curved types, they're just not expensive enough, and there aren't any Rembrandts among the stolen artwork."

"You believe they're just being opportunistic with homeowners away?"

"Leaning that way, but they're armed, clouding the situation."

"You have to wrap this case up, fast. I have enough to deal with."

TAKING the stairs down to my office, I considered what move to take next. Pushing through the stairwell door, my cell rang. The call was coming in from Palm Shores. It had to be the woman Yolanda Sykes said to speak to.

"Detective Luca."

"Hi, I'm Jenny Goodwell. You left a message for me?"

"Yes. Can you talk freely?"

"Yes, I'm by myself in the nursing office."

"Mrs. Sykes mentioned that you were concerned about some of the things going on there. Can you fill me in?"

"I don't want to get in trouble. I need this job."

"This is a confidential conversation. Don't worry, no one will know. What's bothering you?"

"Well, I knew Yolanda's mother and Bill Coby. They were in excellent health when they died."

"I'm sorry, are you a nurse?"

"No, a nurse's aide."

"That's fine. Go ahead."

"Something isn't right, but I can't put my finger on it."

"I see."

"This place is all about the money. Everything Morley does, and Hall too, revolves around making money."

"Who are Morley and Hall?"

"Fred Morley owns the place, and Ryan Hall is his marketing guy."

"Is there something financial or otherwise that was done that could lead to a death?"

"I'm sure there is. I wouldn't put it past them."

She had nothing more tangible than a whisper of smoke.

7

WHEN I GRILLED, I ALWAYS PUT THE NEWS ON, BUT THE nonstop coverage of the coming election had me reaching for the remote. I was about to change channels when the anchor mentioned a decision had been made on the Hollywood Hills nursing home case.

The screen shifted to a video of Hurricane Irma. Large pieces of debris flew past U-shaped palm trees. Flooded streets and pounding waves morphed into an image of the rehabilitation center. The newscaster said, "In a case drawing national attention, a final decision to revoke the license of the nursing home where twelve residents died in 2017 was made today. The Agency for Health Care Administration backed a judge's recommendation. Former Governor Scott had revoked the nursing home's license, but the owners challenged the decision, suing for reinstatement. Today's ruling rejected their appeal to continue operations."

Pictures of rain-soaked residents being wheeled out of the facility rolled across the screen as the anchor continued. "During Hurricane Irma, the rehabilitation center lost power to its air-conditioning. Eventually, the residents were evacuated to a hospital across the street. However, twelve residents later died at that hospital. Nine of those deaths were attributed to heat exposure. The deaths led Governor Scott to mandate every facility have a generator and three days' worth of fuel to power them."

Since Ronnie had approached with concerns about his dad's death, it seemed that issues dealing with the elderly were cropping up left and right. Yesterday's paper had a piece about a homicide in St. Augustine that took place in the main room of an assisted living place.

The article detailed the beating of a seventy-one-year-old resident by another resident, who was eighty-four. The attacker repeatedly struck the younger man about the head and face, killing him in a room filled with residents and staff. The St. Augustine police took the assailant into custody, charging him with murder.

Were incidents concerning facilities housing the elderly becoming more frequent, or was I just tuned into the subject matter? While this was not like the claims being made by Ronnie and others about Palm Shores, it did evidence a lack of security and concern for residents' well being.

TUCKING the box under my arm, I headed to see Dr. Bilotti. He'd been good to me, taking the time and interest to introduce me to wines I'd never heard of. I stopped counting the number of bottles he'd given me. It was time to reciprocate.

Shopping in Costco, I saw a display for Dom Perignon champagne. It came in a fancy box, and the signage said it made a great gift. I thought of Bilotti immediately, and even though it was expensive at a hundred and seventy dollars, I bought a bottle.

The medical examiner was on the phone. The wine-country pictures lining his office would make anyone want to visit. Based on the barrage of medical terms I heard, he must have been talking with another doctor. Staring at a new photo of a conveyor belt full of grapes, I heard him hang up.

"You like that shot? The owner of Morlet Wines sent it to me. He was born in Champagne, France, and his family still makes bubbly over there."

I put the bottle of Dom Perignon on his desk. "Speaking of champagne."

"What's this?"

"It's for you."

"What did you do that for?"

"Come on, Doc, you've given me a ton of bottles."

"Hey, that's what wine lovers do. We share."

"I wouldn't risk getting you a bottle of vino. When I saw this, it seemed perfect."

"Thanks, but it's not necessary."

"How are you doing?"

"Good. I looked over the documents on the woman who died. What's the story behind it?"

"Her daughter is claiming that she was killed by the assisted living place where she was living. Is there anything to support that?"

"She was in good health for a seventy-nine-year-old. No disease or illness that would have seemed to cause death."

"She just died like that?" I snapped my fingers.

"It's not that simple. The death certificate lists acute cardiac syndrome, a catchall for a heart giving out. Without an autopsy, it's impossible to be definitive."

"Wouldn't a death of a seemingly healthy woman require reporting to you, as the medical examiner?"

He leaned back in his chair. "In a perfect world, yes. I'd

examine the body and decide whether to perform an autopsy to determine if there was foul play. However, we don't have the resources for that. We've come to rely on the doctors who were caring for the deceased and the facilities, like Palm Shores, where they live. If they report anything suspicious, we act."

"That's sounds a bit backward."

"It might be, but that's how it's done. And it's not just Collier who does it that way."

"Is it because of their age?"

"I'd be lying if I said it wasn't a factor. Most of the cases involve people in their eighties and nineties, and at that biological age, issues contributing to death are numerous and common."

"I get it, but I don't like the justification, Doc."

"It's not the clinical way to handle it, but with over a thousand deaths a year in the county and one medical examiner, we have to prioritize."

He was right, to a degree. "Do you know this Dr. Krieger at Palm Shores? He signed the death certificate."

"Not really, but the way it works in reality, it's usually a nurse practitioner or an APRN who sees the body and certifies it on the doctor's behalf."

"Ever see anything suspicious in that kind of an arrangement?"

"No, you have to keep in mind the deaths I'm referring to are occurring in nursing homes and assisted living facilities."

"Don't take this the wrong way, Doc, but it sounds like if you're old and in a nursing home and die, we don't scrutinize it."

"Come on, Frank, you know better than that. If there are suspicions of any kind, we take immediate custody of the body until we can determine if foul play was involved."

"How many cases a year like that?"

"A handful."

"I'd like to send over a couple more files for you to look over. Is that okay?"

"Sure, but would you like to tell me what you're looking for?"

"Tell you the truth, Doc, I'm not sure myself."

Heading back to my office, I knew what I really wanted; I needed confirmation that nothing was going on—that the elderly were not being killed by the people in charge of caring for them. I felt a duty to be sure these defenseless and trusting people, in the twilight of their lives, were not in danger, regardless of the motive.

I had to ensure that the world Jessie would inherit was one that took care of its seniors. A place where grandparents, veterans, and those who built this country were respected and treasured. There was no magic wand, but I had to do whatever I could to make sure it happened.

8

———

After flipping through both files, I packaged up the medical records for Bill Coby and John Martin. Nothing seemed to indicate either of them had health issues. If Dr. Bilotti couldn't find anything to explain their deaths, I would have a decision to make.

Fingers crossed that nothing sinister was going on, I dropped the packet in the intercounty mail bin and headed to my office.

Derrick was taking his jacket off and said, "You ever go into any of those galleries in the art district?"

"I like art as much as the next guy, but I stay away from those places. If I wanted an expensive hobby, I'd get a boat."

"I went back today. They're kind of cool. At some of these places, the artist actually works there. I met a couple of them, and from the looks of it, they aren't making any money. Most of them seemed like regular people trying to make a living."

"Not like on TV, huh? No glamor. I saw this documentary on a painter. He was one of those modern guys and popular. He was getting hundreds of thousands for his stuff, but the guy was like a hermit. He spent all his time in a barn he made into a studio, and it was a mess."

"I don't know, I liked being right where they create. You have to wonder where they get the ideas to paint some of the things they do. This one lady had a big yellow square with two squiggly lines running through it. When I first saw it, it seemed like nothing, but it was actually pretty cool."

"You going to start taking lessons?"

"You poking fun?"

"No, I mean it. If you enjoy it, take a shot at it. It'd be a good outlet for you and a helluva lot different than this."

"Maybe one of these days."

"Don't wait too long. Now, did you get anything from your field trip?"

"Nah, the only thing that didn't make sense was at this place The Visual Universe. The place was tiny. It had just eight pieces hanging in a showroom, but it was the place that everyone bought the most from." He flipped through his notebook. "Pierre Robard owns it. He was painting this gigantic painting in the back room. Guy said he does a lot of wholesale business."

"I went to school with a guy named Peter Robard. This guy probably has a good reputation, or, better yet, good prices."

"His store was a bit of a shithole. I'm surprised people with money go into some of these places."

"Maybe they're looking for a bit of authenticity. It'll give them something to talk about at a cocktail party." I used a falsetto voice. "You should have seen where Carl and I were yesterday; it was amazing. I'm telling you, this painter is a creative genius."

"You're a nut, you know that?"

"If we don't laugh a little, we'll end up crying. Look, I

don't know, maybe it's a vendetta kind of thing. Last night, I was rolling this around, and what's being taken just doesn't seem valuable enough to justify the risk. Addicts do stuff like this. These guys are clean and they're armed. What the hell are they trying to do?"

"Revenge? You'd think they'd destroy the places if they wanted to send a message."

"I know. But it just doesn't make sense. They're breaking into empty homes with three guys minimum. They're not going to get more than a thousand fencing what they stole. That's a couple a hundred a man. It doesn't square with the risk."

"Could be kids."

"Not according to the couple who were pistol-whipped."

"What are you thinking?"

"Root around the backgrounds of the homeowners. Maybe there's a thread that links all of them."

THE HOUSE WAS QUIET. It looked like I was going to miss the highlight of most of my days—Jessie running down the hall to greet me. I thought they might have been on the lanai, but I spotted a pair of feet at the end of the couch.

Jessie was nestled into her mother. They were both sleeping. It was as serene a scene as you could imagine, but as I tiptoed to the bedroom, I wondered if motherhood was catching up with Mary Ann. It was the third time that week she'd taken a nap before dinner.

Coming off the bedroom rug onto the tiled living room, my shoes squeaked. Mary Ann woke up.

"Sorry."

"It's okay. I have to get dinner going."

I scooped Jessie up and gave her a wake-up kiss. "How you doing, princess?"

"Hi, Daddy."

"You want to help me water the flowers?"

"Yeah!"

"Get some shoes on first."

Jessie padded to her bedroom, and I said, "You feeling okay?"

"Yeah, just tired."

"Maybe you should cut back on your hours."

"We need the money, Frank."

"I know, but I'm worried about you. You're tired all the time and tripping left and right."

"I'm okay."

"Why don't you get it checked out? Go see the doctor. Maybe it's a vitamin deficiency."

"I'm fine. Stop worrying. It's just a couple of naps; plenty of people take them."

"I know, but we got to be careful. If you're sleeping, Jessie can get into trouble in a heartbeat."

My interviewing skills paid a dividend. "I'll go to see Dr. Finley if it'll make you happy. Okay?"

"Thanks."

It wasn't just Jessie I was worried about. I couldn't put my finger on it, but over the last month, the feeling had been growing that something was wrong with my wife. Making little jokes about her tripping and going to bed at nine could no longer put my mind at ease.

It was true that at times I was a worrywart, and I wasn't a doctor, but there weren't many people better at putting clues together. I was hoping that my fears were driven by love and not reality.

9

MY CELL VIBRATED. IT WAS BILOTTI.

"How are you, Doc?"

"It's going good. How are your girls?"

"All's well. Jessie is going into first grade. It's crazy. I feel like we just took her home from the hospital."

"Enjoy the ride; it's a quick one."

"I'm trying. I told Mary Ann the other day, we got to make the most of each day."

"You're right. With my kids long gone, my motto is a day without wine is a wasted day."

We both laughed. "I don't think Mary Ann is ready for that yet."

"Neither was Kathy. How is Mary Ann doing?"

"You know, I was going to ask you about her."

"What's going on?"

"I don't know, but she's tired all the time and kind of clumsier than she used to be."

"Is she going to see her doctor?"

"Yeah. I pushed her to go."

"That's good."

"Do you have any idea what it might be?"

"It's impossible to say with what you've said. Let her see the doctor and take it from there. I'm sure she's going to be fine. Maybe she's a bit anemic."

"That'd be good. She could just take some iron pills."

"As long as there's not an underlying problem, like internal bleeding."

"She could be bleeding inside?"

"Hold on, it's just a possibility. Has she mentioned finding any blood in her stool?"

"No, she never said anything like that."

"Then it's probably not happening. Let her see the doctor. Okay?"

"Okay."

"Look, I read the files you sent over."

"You find anything?"

"Nothing chronic in either of them. For their ages, both were in excellent health."

"How could they have died so suddenly?"

"Most likely a cardiac event of some type. There was no evidence of heart disease in the records, but something could have been festering."

"And the heart just gave out? Just like that?"

"There are only so many beats in every heart. Just hope you have one with a deep inventory."

"That makes three people with unexplained deaths."

"Keep in mind, they were in their eighties. The explanation is normal aging."

"But you said they were in excellent health."

"They were. You're suspecting foul play, correct?"

"All of them were residents of the same facility."

"Which one?"

"Palm Shores."

AFTER DINNER, I walked a couple of houses down to Ronnie's. A light breeze was blowing, and the sky was streaked with red.

"Hey, Ronnie. Got a couple of minutes?"

"Sure. Come on in. We just finished eating. You want a beer or something?"

They had the same floor plan as we did but it was flipped. His garage and kitchen were on the left and ours to the right. I'd been there hundreds of times, but it still felt weird.

"I'm okay." I said hello to his wife, and we sat around an outside table I helped him pick up from Costco.

"What's up?"

"I wanted to update you on what you asked me to look into. Our medical examiner did me a favor and reviewed your father's medical records. He confirmed what you said about him being in good health."

"I told you."

"I also spoke with Mr. Martin, and he gave me another contact: a woman who believes her mother was killed because she went on Medicaid."

"That's crazy."

"I had the same reaction. The problem is, there's nothing for me to go to the sheriff with. I can't just start a homicide investigation without evidence a crime has been committed."

"Then how do you explain him dying just like that? And Martin's dad?"

"I can't. It can be nothing more than an unfortunate heart attack. I know he was in good shape, but don't forget, he was in his eighties."

"I know how old he was, but I also know he didn't die from a heart attack."

"I'm sorry, pal. I wish there was more I could do to help clear this up. I really do."

"I can't let them get away with it."

At this point, it wasn't clear there was a them or an it. "I understand you're frustrated."

"If you were me, what would you do? I can't sit around and wait for them to kill somebody else's father."

"The reality is that if someone else was murdered, without a confession that they also killed your dad, there'd be nothing to link the cases."

"You know, I can't sleep. I'm the one who suggested he move there, and when he balked at the expense, I convinced him it was worth it."

"It's not your fault, Ronnie."

He hung his head. "Well, it feels like it is. My whole life he looked after me. If I had anything to do, he was always there to help me. I let him down, man."

"Don't beat yourself up. There's no proof anything happened."

"I gotta know for sure. I can't live like this without knowing."

"The only way to do that is messy."

"What do you mean?"

"It'd require an exhumation and an autopsy."

"How could they tell if he was murdered?"

"They examine the organs to see if anything unnatural occurred. Plus they run a series of toxicology tests to see if there are foreign substances."

"I think I should do it."

"It's a tough thing to go through. You should really think about this."

"No. I want to do it. I have to do it. How would I go about doing something like this?"

"There's a company up in Tampa called A Private Autopsy. But first, you'd have to get an approval for the exhumation. I'd start with the health department, but I'm pretty sure a judge has to sign off on it. Your brother would have to be on board. If he contests it, you won't get an approval."

"He's as mad as I am about this. He's not going to be a problem."

"Don't rush into something like this, pal. Take some time and think about it."

"That's all I've been doing is thinking. I'm going to do it and find out, once and for all."

I left Ronnie's feeling uneasy. The emotional roller coaster he and his family were about to embark on was going to be rough. Walking back home, I realized they'd bounce back in time, but what made my stomach clench was the possibility they'd find something.

The implications that one of society's most sacred covenants, to take care of the elderly, was being trashed scared the hell out of me. As my garage door rolled open, I questioned the wisdom of telling Ronnie about an autopsy.

10

I PULLED ONTO THE GRASS AND PARKED. JESSIE SAID, "Is there rides at the fair?"

Mary Ann said, "Jessica, the proper way to say it is, are there rides at the fair?"

"Okay, Mommy. But are there going to be rides?"

"I don't know, honey. But there's a petting zoo, and I bet you can feed a lamb."

"Remember when the big lamb took the bottle, Mommy? He was mean."

"Yes, he was."

I opened the back door and said, "He almost knocked you over. You have to be careful with all animals, Jessie. They don't think like we do; they just react."

"What do you mean, Daddy?"

Lifting her out of her car seat, I said, "When they see food, they just go for it; they don't wait their turn. It's the way God made them, so they can survive when they're in the wild."

As we walked toward the Third Avenue street fair, I

pointed to a vendor selling cotton candy. "Who wants one of those?"

"We just got here, Frank. Let's eat something first."

I rolled my eyes, and Jessie smiled at me. She knew I'd make sure she'd get one before we left. Putting Jessie on my shoulders, we weaved our way through streets crowded with people and stalls selling crafts.

"Look, Daddy."

She pointed to a juggler tossing bowling pins in the air. Heading toward him, I wondered how he learned to do that. Watching him cycle through a half-dozen apples, I noticed a series of booths selling art. A banner with the name Visual Universe caught my eye.

"Hey, Jessie, you want to go over there? People are painting pictures. Real artists."

"Yay! I can help them."

We approached a three-sided tent holding six paintings. Jessie and Mary Ann went to the rear of the tent where a woman was painting at an easel.

I took a closer look at the hanging paintings. They were contemporary but gave off a dark vibe. All were signed by Pierre Robard, the owner of Visual Universe. Joining my girls at the easel, I wondered if Pierre was related to my old schoolmate.

She was painting a sandy beach scene. I said, "That's very different than the rest of the ones here."

She smiled. "I'm fascinated with capturing what I see in nature. Pierre, he's super contemporary."

"You work for him?"

"No, I'm just manning the booth for him." She looked at Jessie and said, "Would you like to help me?"

"Oh yeah. Mommy, can I help?"

"Yes, but don't get any paint on you."

"Don't worry, I have a smock and gloves for her. Come over here."

THE SMELL of a dark roasted coffee perked me up. Sure enough, a Starbucks cup was sitting in the center of my desk.

"Morning." I picked up the cup. "Thanks, partner."

"Morning. How was the Third Avenue fair?"

"Crowded. Jessie had a ball. Oh, that gallery, Visual Universe, they had a booth, and the woman there was unbelievable. She let Jessie paint with her. She liked it so much, I thought she was going to burst."

"Sounds like fun, maybe she should take painting lessons."

"We'll see. Robard wasn't there, but the owner had some of his pieces on display. He wanted six to seven hundred each."

"He was working on a huge piece when I saw him."

"Didn't you say he did a lot of wholesale business?"

"Yeah, it was a small place."

I went to hit the tab for my email box and saw the one for the DMV portal. Opening the interagency site, I typed in Pierre Robard.

A man with a shaved head and a soul patch appeared beside his vitals. Robard was forty-six, brown eyed, and an even six foot. He liked to drive fast and owned a 2014 Porsche 911. Though it was six years old, it wasn't your starving artist type of vehicle.

I like to think it was intuition, but it could have been habit that made me punch Robard's name into the NCIC database. The results from the nation's crime center sent a shot of coffee-laced acid to the back of my throat.

Pierre Robard had been arrested in Santa Monica for art forgery in October of 2012. The charges were dropped. Robard claimed he was unaware the artwork he was selling was forged.

"We might have a lead on the burglaries. Robard was arrested in California for art forgery."

"What?"

"The charges were dropped. He claimed he didn't know the works were forged. It's too early to call the detective who handled it, but it's something we need to check into."

Resisting the urge to jump in the car and visit Pierre Robard at his business, I focused on dealing with my emails. It took me a solid ninety minutes.

Hoping Detective Morales had the early shift, I called the Santa Monica Police at five after eleven. They passed me to the Criminal Investigative Division.

Morales answered the phone, and after introducing myself, I explained why I was calling.

"Yeah, I remember that one. Those guys were pretty slick. Two of them were knocking off paintings, and Robard was peddling them from a storefront on Wilshire Boulevard. The place is a taco joint now."

"Why were the charges dropped?"

"The DA didn't want to go to trial. The other two pled guilty, but Robard stuck to his story, and they let him off. I didn't agree, but that's above my pay grade."

"So, you believed Robard played a larger role than he'd admitted?"

"No doubt in my mind. You see, the others were, you know, those arty types. The copies they made were unreal. I don't know anything about painting, but they were exact duplicates. But those guys lacked communication skills. There's no way they could have sold them without Robard."

"How did you get wind of the scam?"

"We got a tip from someone who'd been in Robard's place. This guy was shopping with his wife and knew his stuff. These guys weren't pushing, like, Picassos or anything, they were lesser-known pieces that only people who are into art would know. This guy knew there was something funky going on 'cause he saw one of the paintings in a gallery in New York."

"How long was it going on?"

"We think it was about two years, just after Robard leased the storefront. This could've been going on somewhere else beforehand. I mean, if these guys were smart, they'd move around. You know what I mean?"

"Sure, makes sense. How did the buyers react? Did anybody file a civil complaint and sue?"

"Nah, they were embarrassed and wanted it hushed up. They all knew something was wrong. Who knows what the paintings were really worth? But from what I was able to find out, the prices they were selling at were a third of what they should have been."

Everybody loves a bargain. "They must have thought they were stolen, then."

"That's what I figured."

"Can you do me a favor and send me the case file?"

"Sure, make the request on the portal, and I'll jump right on it."

11

———

THE SKY WAS AS BLUE AS IT GOT. NOT A CLOUD IN SIGHT, and the humidity was low for June. Contemplating the odds of a cooler summer, I made my way to the office. Things were quiet. A bit too much so.

It had been a month since the house bandits had struck. Why had they suddenly stopped? It defied logic. As June wore on, more people left town, leaving hundreds more targets to strike. And they were more vulnerable as fewer neighbors were around to report unusual activity.

One of the lesser-known secrets of policing was our reliance on offenders continuing to do what they did. With every violation, the chances of catching them increased. It made it easier. Either they'd screw up eventually, or we'd detect a pattern that would lead us to the perps.

Criminals, especially gangs, rarely quit while ahead. They'd go underground after a big score or when the heat was on, but would always resurface when they felt it was safe. What had driven these thieves to lay low?

We had run down all the service companies the homes used. Had we touched a nerve at one of them? There were three landscapers, two pool companies, and a pest outfit that we looked into. Had checking under one of those rocks been the reason? None of the companies serviced all the homes, but all were in each of the neighborhoods.

Sipping coffee, I opened my email box. More evidence of how slow it was, only twenty-eight had come in. It took me an hour to reply to all of them. Then I fished the report on yesterday's arrests out of the paperwork on my desk.

There were eight arrests. None of the names rang a bell. I pulled my ringing cell phone out of my pocket, thinking if it slowed down anymore, my job would be in danger. It was my neighbor Ronnie.

"Hey, Ronnie, how are you?"

"Look, we got the autopsy results."

I held my breath.

"They found a drug, some kind of hypnotic one, like that date-rape drug."

"Rohypnol?"

"I don't know."

"And that was the cause of his death?"

"Yeah, they killed him. I can't believe it. Who would do something like that? And why? It doesn't make sense."

"If they did, we'll get them. Trust me. I'll make them pay."

"You really think you'll find who did it?"

"No doubt. I need that report ASAP."

"I got it in an attachment. I'll forward it now."

"Good. I'll get back to you. Do me a favor. Don't mention this to John Martin or anyone connected to Palm Shores."

I kept hitting refresh until the email arrived. The attachment was lengthy. I hit print and paged to the cause of death. It was an overdose of a benzodiazepine. The presence of the amino flunitrazepam was found in the filtering organs, the liver and the kidneys, as well as the heart.

I plugged the drug names into the search bar. The date-rape drug, Rohypnol, appeared in four of the five top results. Reading through an article, I remembered Derrick saying he had experience with this crap while he was in DC. When I read the sentence that the elderly should not be administered this drug, I got up and marched upstairs.

THE SHERIFF'S secretary knocked on his door and told him I needed to speak with him. I saw Chester hesitate before nodding, and I entered.

"I'm sorry, sir, but this couldn't wait."

He took his readers off. "What's going on, Frank?"

"I wanted to discuss opening a homicide investigation, and it may involve Palm Shores."

"The fancy retirement place?"

"Yes, sir."

"Sit down. Tell me what's going on."

"A neighbor's father moved into Palm Shores. I actually helped move him in. He passed away shortly after moving in, from what they termed a natural death. He was in his eighties but was in better shape than me. His family was upset and came to me with suspicions that their father had been murdered. I told him there was nothing I could do, but he gave me another family who'd lost their father as well. I talked with him as well, just to hear him out, but there was nothing obvious there. He gives me a woman who claimed her mother was murdered because she was going on to Medicaid."

"You're losing me. What's the motivation for a place to murder its residents?"

"Money. Both men bought units that are sold back to the facility at a discount at death."

His shoulders sagged. "Jesus Christ."

"I know, sir. None of the bodies were autopsied at death. There was nothing concrete. I told my neighbor the only way forward was to privately exhume his father and have an autopsy performed. The results just came in. The man was killed by an overdose of a heavy sedative, like the ones used in date rapes."

He wagged his head. "This is terrible. But there's no proof it was the facility itself. It could have been anyone, even the family, for God's sake."

"I'm not jumping to any conclusions, sir. That's what I know at this point."

"Open a case and find out what happened. But keep this quiet."

"Thank you, sir. I'm going to need your support."

"Of course. We can't have our seniors being murdered in places they're supposed to be safe in."

"What I'd like to do is exhume the other two bodies and test them. If they come up positive, we know we have a serial killer on our hands. Corporate or otherwise."

Chester's face lost a shade of color. Most people would have thought it was the idea of a serial killer, but I knew it was the exhumation that gave him the willies. "One step at a time, Frank."

"I understand, sir, but I'm looking at the time element. We can get an order signed off quickly and have Dr. Bilotti do the autopsy."

"We can't be rushing into this. Exhumations are emotional."

A little bit of reaching was called for. "The other families are prepared to act privately, sir. And they're the type that would make noise, especially the lady. She was ready to go to the media when I talked to her."

"Slow it down, Luca. You barge in here with scant evidence and expect me to order a double exhumation?"

"I know you value speed, sir, and this is as delicate a case as we've ever had. We have many assisted living places in the county. I wouldn't want this to become a bigger story than it is."

"At this point, you need to get an investigation going. In the meantime, I'll consider your request."

"Thank you, sir. If you don't mind, I'll get the necessary paperwork if you decide to go ahead with it."

12

———

After bringing Derrick up to speed, I said, "Tell me what you know about this Rohypnol drug."

"It's the preferred drug of bastards who target girls in bars to rape. It's odorless, and most of the legit stuff turns blue when it's put into a liquid to alert people, but all the off-line stuff doesn't throw a color."

"What do they use this stuff for in the first place?"

"It's used in some countries to treat severe insomnia and as an aid for anesthesia."

"It works fast, doesn't it?"

"Yeah, you know, in Sweden, it's the second-most common drug used in suicides. Once you take a lethal dose, there's virtually no way of coming back."

"I can't see a killer using a pill form, unless they swap it for something a person is taking already. Getting someone to drink something that's been laced is dangerous. I'm leaning toward an injection."

"It'd be quick. The killer puts a hand or pillow over the victim's mouth and sticks them with a needle."

"That would leave a mark, but if they believe an autopsy is not going to happen . . ."

"Or maybe the victim gets regular injections of some kind, and he inserts it in the same area."

"If a victim is awake, they'd resist. It's more likely he'd plunge a needle into a leg or maybe the gut area. We need to ask Bilotti how quick it would work in a scenario like that."

"If it's ingested, it takes fifteen to twenty minutes. But if the dose is large enough to kill, it'd be faster."

"We'll sort that out. What we need to do is develop background on Bill Coby. I know the family, so I'd rather you handle that. You can press where it may be uncomfortable. Find out all you can. Who he was close with, who he had battles with, who visited him, you know the drill. The family thinks it was Palm Shores who killed him, but for all we know, it could have been a family member who stood to inherit what he had."

"Or some nut with an agenda. I was reading something about a group of millennials that formed an organization to fight seniors. They feel too much money and resources are being used by baby boomers. They even espoused euthanasia when a person hits eighty-five."

"You can't make this crap up."

"They said Social Security was going broke because of the boomers."

"They paid into the system; they're just getting back the money they put in."

"I hear you."

"We need a list of everyone who worked at Palm Shores as well. It could be someone like that New Jersey nurse that killed forty people at the hospital where he worked."

"The worst one was that German nurse. He killed, like, eighty-five patients."

"How nobody noticed a pattern depresses the hell out of me."

"We'd never miss anything like that."

I agreed, even though I knew I was the furthest from infallibility. The talk about a serial killer unsettled me. If true, time was an enemy. I told Derrick I'd be back in an hour.

JUST PAST GOLDEN GATE BOULEVARD, I turned off Forty-One into Vision Works' parking lot. The store was the largest eyeglass place I'd ever seen. Two salespeople were showing clients an eye-numbing number of frame choices. Ronnie was behind a desk at the rear of the store.

We exchanged a handshake. I said, "Can you talk?"

"Sure. What's going on?"

I looked around. No one within earshot. "This has got to be kept confidential."

"No worries."

Maybe it was an appropriate reply, but it was another saying, like "no problem," that was overused to the point of annoyance. "I asked you to keep the autopsy results quiet."

"I didn't tell anyone."

I lowered my voice further. "Here's the thing. I think the fastest way to move on this is to leak the results to the press. The pressure will force the sheriff to move on exhuming other possible victims."

"You want me to go to the *Daily News*?"

"You could. *Wink News* would be better; it'll hit the air fast."

"I never did something like this."

"You can't say anything about your belief it was Palm Shores. Not only could it hurt the investigation, you could open yourself up to a defamation suit. We don't know who did it at this point."

"I could get sued?"

"It's nothing to be concerned about as long as you don't speculate on who did it. You call them and tell them your father died, and the autopsy proved it wasn't a natural death. Tell them a lethal drug was found in his body and that's that. Nothing more."

"Aren't they going to want more than that?

"Believe me, that's enough. They're going to be thrilled to run something big like this."

"No problem. I'll do it."

"You have to wait until I tell you. Okay?"

"Sure."

"I'll let you know."

"All right."

"You sell those things that keep your sunglasses in place?"

"Sure. We have a rack full of them over there."

"Good. I don't want to walk out of here with nothing."

It was a risky move, but I knew Chester. He'd delay making a decision until forced to. By that time, another defenseless senior could be lying on a slab. I wanted the county to support the exhumation. That way, it would be approved faster than a private request. Especially when we tagged it as a possible homicide.

I wanted everything in motion but wanted to sniff around Palm Shores before the news broke. It would provide a before-and-after perspective that could be useful as the investigation unfolded.

13

————

BEAUTIFUL BEGONIAS INTERSPERSED WITH ROYAL PALMS lined both sides of Palm Shores entrance. I pulled onto a circular driveway with a large porte cochere.

A handful of residents sat on benches that overlooked a lake with a fountain spraying water. I parked in a visitor space, and before I closed the door to the Cherokee received two "good mornings" from employees in white shirts embroidered with palm tree logos. My knowledge of these types of facilities was limited. Approaching the entrance, I recalled a husband of one of Mary Ann's friends ran a place called The Beach House. I'd have to reach out for a quick education.

When the second set of sliders opened, I did a double take. A Welcome to Palm Shores sign, with my name on it, sat next to the receptionist's desk. I'd called less than twenty minutes ago. I checked in, declined an offer of something to drink, and drifted to a map of Palm Shores hanging on the wall. This place was large and meandering.

The main part of the complex was organized in a wide, angular U-shape, with the reception and main gathering space at the bottom. Four rectangular buildings topped the complex, and six others were scattered near recreational areas.

A pair of structures named Gulf Towers were the farthest from reception. I was betting, with their view, they were also the most expensive units in the community.

"Mr. Luca, welcome to Palm Shores. I'm Fred Morley, the managing partner."

He extended his hand. Wearing a blue, double-breasted blazer and tan slacks, he looked like he belonged on a cruise ship. Sending someone this high level to meet me was a discerning signal.

"Nice to meet you. I didn't realize how large a facility this was."

He cringed at the word facility. "We're proud that six hundred and forty-three residents call Palm Shores home. Let's head to my office."

Morley's office was a handful of rooms away from the lobby but featured a wall of glass overlooking a flower-filled garden. Four chairs fronted his desk, and to the left sat a couch and a pair of wing chairs. He swung around his desk.

"How can I help the sheriff's office?"

"We're conducting an investigation. It's preliminary at this point. We wanted to alert you that we'd be talking to some of the people that live and work here."

"What's the nature of this investigation?"

"I'm not at liberty to discuss an active case, Mr. Morley."

"Does it involve someone on our staff or a resident?"

"I can't answer that at this point. As soon as I am able to disclose information, I will."

"Is this related to an oversight of Palm Shores? Because we have an impeccable record with the Department of Elder Affairs."

"I'm aware of your nursing home's record. Can you

provide a breakdown of what kinds of residents you have? Whether they are independent, assisted, or require nursing care."

"We're not a nursing home." He let that sit for a second before continuing. "Over ninety percent of our residents live either independently—"

"What percentage are private pay?"

"Upwards of ninety-five percent."

"That seems high."

"Palm Shores' residents enjoy the most elaborate array of recreational choices you'll find in Southwest Florida. We have a golf course, putting greens, three swimming pools, five miles of walking and biking trails, a bowling alley, bocce courts, tennis and pickleball, among others. Our culinary team is the finest in the county. All these amenities and services have costs. We simply can't operate at our level at Medicaid reimbursement rates. If we did something like that, we'd ruin the experience for everyone."

"What about your competitors? What are their ratios?"

"We don't have competitors. Palm Shores is in a class all its own."

"How does one become a resident?"

"We're selective. We want to make sure there's a good fit. There's a meeting with the prospect and their family where we discuss—"

"I was referring to what it costs. I understand you have different models."

"Oh, yes. It's dependent on the prospective resident. We offer a menu of options to choose from. Some residents prefer to enjoy all their meals in one of our dining rooms, while others choose less frequent visits. Then there are the levels of assistance some require. If they need help with their medications or showering, dressing, those sorts of daily tasks—"

"And each level costs more?"

"Filling a resident's needs requires manpower and resources."

"I understand you also sell units to residents."

"Yes, we make that available, but it's technically not a sale."

"How does that work?"

"Some residents prefer to pay for their living quarters in a lump sum and enjoy reduced monthly maintenance fees."

"What if they move out?"

"Well, we rarely have someone leave. But if they did, they'd get a partial refund."

"I see. How many doctors and nurses do you have?"

"We employ a full-time doctor, and there are head nurses in each division, one of whom is a practitioner."

"Business good?"

"We're a private enterprise."

"You're a partner, right?"

"Yes, everything I have is invested in Palm Shores. We've created a unique environment for seniors to be engaged with one another, remain active, and continue to grow."

The way he said it made me wish I was in my eighties. "I'd like to take a walk around."

He stood. "Sure, I'll show you around."

"That's not necessary. I'd rather be on my own."

"Let me get you a golf cart."

"I don't need one."

"If you're going to the towers you will, it's a half mile from here."

I hadn't driven a golf cart since right after I moved to Naples. It was the one and only time I played golf. Morley was right. Between the size of this place and a rising sun, a cart was the way to get around.

The pathways were wide and clearly marked, with one side wide enough for two carts and the other for pedestrians and bikers. I was surprised by the number of people out and about. Six tennis courts were occupied with doubles players, and a pair of pickleball courts were in action.

Palm Shores' grounds were well maintained but not elaborately planted like the entrance. At the end of the main structure were a series of one-story buildings housing coach homes. All had driveways and a third of them garages.

I weaved my way through four buildings that were six stories high. Each of the units had small terraces. Steps away from the area, a boardwalk led to a wide canal where a pair of boats gently bobbed.

Wondering if prices rose the farther you got from the main building, I headed toward the towers. Slowing my cart down, I looked up at the tower to the left. It was where Ronnie's father had lived.

14

"Daddy's home!" Jessie ran down the hallway to meet me.

The smell of thyme, or was it rosemary, was in the air. "How's my princess doing?"

"Mommy said we can go in the pool before we eat."

I didn't want to do anything but sit and sip a glass of wine. "Sure, sunshine. Let me say hello to Mommy, then I'll get changed."

I kissed Mary Ann on the cheek. She smelled like Ivory soap.

"She's been waiting for you to get home."

"We have a new case."

"I heard. Maria told me that her father-in-law was murdered. I can't believe it."

"That's what it looks like. An overdose of a date-rape drug."

"Who would want to harm an eighty-year-old? It's unbelievable."

Jessie came in holding two bathing suits. "Which one, Daddy?"

Wondering what kind of world she was growing up in, I pointed to the yellow one. "That one is perfect. Hurry and get changed, or we won't have enough time to play shark."

She shrieked and ran to her room.

I said, "How can such innocence and evil exist in the same world?"

"How can someone prey on kids or people like Ronnie's dad? It's scary. Since she told me, I can't stop thinking about it."

I had no illusions about what kind of world we lived in. The move to Florida had brightened my disposition, but the sun and sand couldn't erase depravity. There was less of it, but it was there, and having a daughter heightened the threat.

It was usually me who needed reassurance that humanity wasn't descending into darkness, but the look on her face forced a role reversal. "Everything is going to be all right." I put my arms around her.

"Has the world gone crazy?"

"No. We haven't had a homicide in the county in a while. The reality is, it's been quiet, honey."

"You think so? On the news, just before you came in, there's some guy in New York who's raping women in their seventies. You call that quiet?"

It was hard to argue with that kind of degeneracy.

I tightened my arms around her. "Don't worry about stuff like that; that's just New York."

"That's not exactly comforting."

I didn't know where it came from, but something a New Jersey priest had told me popped into my head. I'd expressed an interest in helping homeless women and their children, but after seeing how large a problem it was, I began to reconsider. I paraphrased his advice. "When you go in the water at

Vanderbilt Beach, do you think about how clean the water in Jersey is?"

"You're losing me."

"We swim down here. It's my job to make sure the water is clean. I'm going to do everything and anything to protect my family and our town."

She squeezed me and said, "I know you will."

I pecked her cheek. "I better get changed."

"You don't have much time; I have a chicken in the oven."

"I thought I smelled rosemary."

THOUGH MY PLAN was working like a Swiss watch, I wasn't looking forward to wading through a Chester windstorm. It was good and bad that he was holding a strategy meeting with the political advisers of his reelection campaign. The good part was I didn't get a phone call over the planted news story. On the other side, politics would occupy an even larger slice of the sheriff's mind.

Though the primary was a year away, Chester was the heavy favorite. His challenger was promoting the myth that Collier County had become a police state. I knew some would buy that, but the overwhelming majority knew the county was one of the safest in the nation.

In a blue suit and red tie, Chester looked every bit the politician as he chatted with staffers outside his office. He smiled, and I followed him into his office. The sound of the door closing was still in the air when he said, "How did this get out?"

"I'm not sure, sir."

He hung up his coat. "You told me your neighbor was going to keep it quiet until we were ready to take action."

"He said he didn't say anything."

"Then who was it?"

"It could have been someone at Private Autopsy. I've heard the press pays them for leaks."

He collapsed into his chair. "If there's one thing I dislike, it's surprises. We need to control the flow of information."

"I understand, sir."

"There's going to be pressure to expand the investigation."

Exactly. "We should get ahead of it, sir."

"I'm going to authorize the exhumation and autopsy requests."

"A sound move."

"I don't want this turning into a circus. Something like this could shake the senior community into believing we aren't protecting them. If that thought catches on, I'll be run out of town before the election."

"I don't think that's remotely possible, sir."

"Not possible? Did you see what they did to Remington in Atlanta?"

I had. There'd been an uproar over a white officer shooting a black teenager, who died a day later. It didn't make sense; the kid was armed and had robbed a 7-Eleven. The police commissioner was forced to resign because the community claimed it was an example of his officers using excessive force. "The people of the county are behind you, sir. They know they're lucky to have you."

A smile surfaced on his face but quickly faded. "We'll see about that. The public is fickle—they love you one day, then the next you're the devil. Seniors used to be different. They were loyal, but not anymore. That's what makes a case like this dangerous. If they find a way to blame me, they'll flip on me in a heartbeat."

"I'll make sure we keep it as quiet as possible."

"What I want is a quick resolution. You understand that?"

"Yes, sir."

15

———

I followed Dylan Nealy, the husband of Mary Ann's friend, through a high-ceilinged room featuring an upright piano and a dozen seating areas into a hallway. The Beach House had a decidedly different feel from Palm Shores.

Pulsing Caribbean music was coming out of an area with wood flooring. A semicircle of smiling residents were seated. An instructor, in lime-green tights, led them through a series of exercises.

"Looks like they're having fun."

"Rosie is the best. She's great at getting the older residents involved in activities that get 'em exercise."

"That's fantastic."

"Getting them moving is not only good for their physical well-being, but the connection up here"—he tapped his temple—"is even more important."

Pictures of the facility and residents filled the walls of Nealy's office. I could see my car from his window. It was a stark contrast to Morley's Palm Shores' office.

"I appreciate you taking the time. We're working a case

where a resident of Palm Shores died under suspicious circumstances."

"I know about it. Damn shame, if it's true."

It would be worse than that, but I nodded. "What I need is a primer on these types of places. I need to understand how they operate, and it's not because I think Palm Shores did anything wrong. What I need is an overview that I can filter my investigation through."

"Sure, anything I could do to help. But we're very different types of places."

"In what way?"

"We serve different markets. They cater to the higher-end consumer, kind of like what Grey Oaks did with Moorings Park. We offer more affordable options, and we don't sell units like they do."

"You rent them?"

"We offer multiple floor plans, from a studio up to two bedrooms, and the monthly charge includes meals, assisted living services, but nothing complex, and regularly scheduled activities. We're basically month-to-month. We even have a couple of seasonal residents."

"Can you explain the sales model at Palm Shores?"

"It's not a sale per se. They try to steer residents into putting down a large payment, offering them reduced monthly expenses in exchange. It locks people in, and when they die or leave, they don't get it all back."

"Why would anyone do that?"

"It's a bet they're going to be there long enough to recoup it through lower fees. They make it attractive for people to make the trade. Plus they get a handful of perks for parting with their money."

"How do you handle it when one of your residents goes from privately paying to Medicaid?"

"It's a challenge for everyone in the industry. The payment from Medicaid is below what it costs us on a per capita basis. In our financial models, we built in a populace that includes ten percent on government assistance. We don't go looking for it, but we don't force people out either."

"Palm Shores discourages them?"

"They go further than that. I hear they even pay nursing homes under the table to take anyone who goes on Medicaid."

"Doesn't the patient have a say in it?"

"I've never seen their contracts, but the reality is, the facility doesn't have to keep them. It doesn't look good to the other residents, as most people worry they're going to run out of money, but Palm Shores is within their rights."

"It sounds cruel to move someone out, but I get it; you can't force anyone to lose money."

"It's something we're going to have to confront as a society. There's a huge wave of people who'll likely end up in places like this. And we're living longer with each passing year."

"Life expectancy down here is higher than the national average."

"That's true. The population is aging, but how it's going to be paid for isn't clear."

The question I needed to answer was whether killing off seniors was someone's idea of an answer.

I TAPPED a sheet of paper with my forefinger. "We need to start whittling this list down."

Derrick said, "That's everybody who works at Palm Shores."

"For the moment, let's concentrate on who benefits financially from a scheme to turn over housing at Palm Shores."

"It's pretty obvious: the company itself. They get to keep a nice chunk of money when somebody dies."

"No doubt."

"There's only three owners, so in the case of Bill Coby, that works out to a cool twenty-five grand a partner."

"I'm not saying twenty-five K isn't a lot of money, but they have a nice business. I'm sure they're making a couple of hundred grand a year."

"They must be. The property records value their personal homes at a million and a half to two."

"I wonder what Morley's deal is. The other partners don't get involved in the day-to-day. Morley has to get a bigger slice to compensate."

"Unless they were the money men. Or at least put up more than Morley did to build the place."

"Still, operating partners are usually paid a piece of the profits before the others get anything."

"You're probably right. I can't see how someone who doesn't know the ins and outs of the place, sneaking in and killing."

"Probably right? Did you just say that?"

"Getting touchy, partner?"

"Just busting. If someone like a salesperson worked on commission, they'd have a vested interest in filling"—I fingered quote marks—"vacancies."

"I'm sure they work on commission; everybody in real estate does."

I picked up the list. "There's only one salesman. Guy named Ryan Hall. He's listed as vice president of sales and marketing."

"I'll run him and Morley through the system. See if anything pops up."

"What kinds of names did Ronnie give you?"

"He said his dad just had one male friend and two women at Palm Shores. But he said he was friendly with one of the aides and a maintenance guy. I have their names."

"Let's start with them. But what about the inheritance angle? He give you any idea what his dad was worth, and who stands to get it?"

"Coby was worth about six hundred thousand. Ronnie and his brother are the only heirs."

"His brother lives in Cape Coral, right?"

"Yeah, he teaches in Lee."

I'd seen a dozen murders over a lot less than three hundred thousand, but if it turned out that Ronnie killed his dad, I'd have to ask God for a new set of instincts.

16

THE PALM SHORES RECEPTION AREA WAS A QUIET PLACE TO read. I caught someone approaching out of the corner of my eye and reluctantly put the *Food and Wine* magazine back on the side table. The smiling man heading toward me threw me off.

"Mr. Luca?" He stuck out his hand. "Ryan Hall, it's a pleasure to meet you."

Was it his first name that made me think he looked like Ryan Seacrest? We shook and I said, "You may hear this often, but you look like Ryan Seacrest."

He smiled. "Probably as much as people say you resemble George Clooney."

Hall was wearing a tight-fitting sports jacket and blue suede Gucci loafers. He seemed to have rebounded from the excessive drinking that led to three DUI arrests when he was twenty-eight.

"Not as much as I used to. George is aging a lot better than I am."

"It's his job to look good. I'm sure he has an army helping him look his best."

"Must be nice."

"You don't need the help. You look fantastic."

"I don't know about that."

"Trust me, you do. Now, what can I do for you?"

"I had a couple of questions. Can we go somewhere private?"

"Absolutely! Let's go to my office."

Hall's office had a double window overlooking a lake. A beige couch and a cocktail table lined the left wall. Four armchairs in a semicircle were in front of his desk, and a credenza, stacked with sales brochures, was behind it.

A key fob with a winged emblem sat on his desk. I did a double take. It wasn't for a Genesis; the logo was Bentley's. Hall bounced into his chair, saying, "I'm assuming this concerns Bill Coby."

"Yes."

"He was a nice man. Has a good family too."

"His son is a neighbor of mine."

His face relaxed. "Oh, I get it. He asked you to look into this. I understand now, not that I don't blame him. I'd do the same thing."

There was no need to inform him this was way beyond a neighborly favor.

"What is your role at Palm Shores?"

"Sales and marketing. I show prospects units, give tours of the property, and answer their questions."

"You're the sole person doing that?"

"Yep, the one and only."

"That's surprising, given the size of this place.

"They keep an eye on costs here."

"Sounds like a challenge."

"I don't want to brag, but I keep this place full. They had three people doing what I do before I got here. They didn't know how to close. Most people don't, but it comes naturally to me."

"How do you get compensated?"

"Straight commission against a draw."

"Different rates for those that put money down versus those that pay monthly?"

"Uh, yes, everyone, including the resident, does better when opting for the lower monthly fees."

"What's the difference in commission?"

"Seven versus four percent."

"That's sizable."

"Like I said, we all do better when somebody decides to buy down the fees."

"You mentioned Bill Coby's family. Who did you meet with when he expressed an interest in Palm Shores?"

"The first visit he came with your neighbor, Ronnie. The next time, his other son, Robert, was there."

"Anyone resistant to him moving here?"

"Nothing more than the usual concerns. They all believed he'd be happy here, and he was. He told me several times he enjoyed living at Palm Shores."

"They weren't concerned about the cost?"

"No. It's really not a financial decision but a lifestyle one. I know we have a reputation that we cater to the wealthy, but we're not expensive, especially when you consider how special Palm Shores is."

He was drinking the same Kool Aid as Morley, but as a salesperson, you knew there'd be a spin to anything he said.

"Did either son try to steer Mr. Coby from putting down three hundred thousand dollars?"

"Everyone discusses the pros and cons of going with a straight rental versus the buy-down option."

"I'm interested in what the Coby children said about it."

"Well, I think the younger son, Robert, he tried to convince his father to rent."

"How hard was his attempt?"

"He felt strongly about it."

"Was he angry about it?"

He shrugged. "I excused myself, to allow them privacy to talk it over. It's something I do when these discussions became heated."

"Who was arguing?"

"Mostly Mr. Coby and his son Robert. But I don't make a big deal about it. It's normal for family members to have a range of opinions. I see it all the time."

Family arguments were a regular occurrence. Finding an eighty-five-year-old man filled with an illegal drug was not. We had to look into Coby's younger son and find out how Hall could be tooling around town in a Bentley.

***

I HAD to place three calls into Detective Morales to get the Robard forgery file. His idea of jumping right on it was another example of how much slower things worked on the West Coast. The delay wasn't a problem; the Palm Shores case had moved front and center, and the thieves hadn't struck again.

The file was an interesting read. The more I read, the more I knew, as Morales did, that Robard wasn't innocent. What emerged by reading the file and interviews was a smart, cagey man.

It was as close to victimless as you could get. Robard and his coconspirators targeted people who wanted "one of a kind" art at bargain prices. The genius of the scheme was that these buyers were supposedly sophisticated and eager to get something no one else had at below-market rates. The combination resulted in not only their getting scammed, but reluctant to make noise about it.

The lack of any victim willing to press charges led to the dismissal of charges against Robard and pleas of guilt to retail theft, a misdemeanor, for his accomplices. Robard had gotten as far away from Southern California as possible, moving to Chicago for a year, before ending up in Naples.

Wondering if they had simply relocated their scam, I tracked down his coconspirators, but both still resided in California. There was no doubt that Naples had its share of art lovers and bargain hunters, but what made it ideal for someone like Robard was the abundance of culture pretenders who thought money could buy anything.

If Robard was replaying the Santa Monica scheme, the discounted prices would make it irresistible to those looking to leapfrog the social ladder.

Robard had been in Chicago for only a year. Was it the cold climate or the heat from the police that sent him to Naples? Chicago had plenty of violent crime to deal with. How long would it take for them to catch onto an art scam?

There wasn't anything else in the national database on Robard, leading me to conclude the answer was probably a decade.

17

Lois Gershwin carried herself like she'd walked down hundreds of runways. As the sliders closed behind her, she waved to a pair of women playing checkers. Without slowing down, she took off a pair of sunglasses and put them in her bag.

Her grip was firm and her smile warm. "Nice to meet you, Detective. You remind me of someone. I can't recall who, but it'll come to me."

"I appreciate you taking the time to speak with me. I know you had something planned."

She pointed a finger at me. "George Clooney. That's who you look like. Anyway, I went for a walk this morning instead of taking the water aerobics class."

"There's a lot to do here."

"Many places advertise they're an active community, but this place actually delivers on it. I'm not an elitist, but the fact is, many people in the upper income brackets take better care of themselves and can take advantage of all that Palm Shores has to offer."

"It's certainly not cheap."

"That it isn't. But that's another subject." She sighed. "The news about Bill is very disturbing. He was a wonderful man, a good human being."

"I understand the two of you were close."

"We got along well. He wasn't one of those macho men, and believe me, we have plenty of them here. He was a gentleman." She leaned in. "Never made a pass at me."

Was there a future reality TV show in this place? The way the nation's demographics were trending, it'd be more popular than *The Bachelor*.

"I also knew Mr. Coby. His son Ronnie is a neighbor of mine."

"He's a nice young man."

He was my age, but as Einstein said, everything is relative. "Do you have any idea who would have done this to Bill?"

She shook her head. "I've given it a lot of thought, and I know there's no shortage of rumors, but I believe they're unsubstantiated."

"What kinds of rumors?"

"That Palm Shores is somehow responsible. They had grievance counselors for us, and at a town hall meeting right after the news broke, they denied any responsibility. Maybe I don't want to believe something like that, but I just can't see them hurting their own residents."

She shook her head as a short woman, built like a sumo wrestler, stormed by.

"She works here?"

"No, but she thinks she owns the place."

"She has family here?"

"She's a private aide for Martha Ringer but sticks her nose in everything. To say she is bossy is an understatement."

"What's her name?"

"Galena Vuvich. She's Russian. And very religious."

I jotted down the name. "Is there a pattern you can think of, where, say Bill Coby, Charles Martin, or even Rosa Sykes had an enemy in common or something unusual?"

She raised a hand to her mouth. "You think there's a serial killer in here?"

"I'm sorry to alarm you, but in my business I can't discount any possibility. I'm just doing by job."

"I realize you have to entertain all kinds of scenarios, but the thought of someone doing this is frightening."

"Do you take any medications?"

"Yes. Zocor to help control my cholesterol: it's one forty-nine. Why do you ask?"

"Do you rely on help here to take it each day?"

"Of course not. I can take care of myself."

"I didn't mean to imply otherwise. I was just wondering if someone needed help—"

"For residents that need assistance, the Well-Being Center administers whatever dose is required."

"They make rounds to deliver medications, like in a hospital?"

"Yes, they have a cart with the day's doses. It goes around three times a day. At nine, two, and eight at night."

"Who gives the meds out?"

"One of the aides."

"Who, exactly?"

"Oh my God! You think it could be her?"

"I don't think anything in particular at the moment. The person delivering the meds could be handing out pills that were compromised."

"If it weren't so terrifying, all the possibilities would be fascinating."

What I did for a living had been called many things, but

never fascinating. I made a note of the aide who administered the medicines and got up. "Thank you for allowing me to barge into your day, Ms. Gershwin."

"No trouble at all. Bill was a dear friend, and if I can assist in any way, I consider it my duty to do so."

"Here's my card. If you think of anything or anyone he saw that—"

"You know, Bill had a visitor that day. He wouldn't say who it was, which I thought was strange."

"Doesn't everyone have to sign in?"

"They're supposed to, but the security tends to be more visual than actual."

"It sounds like you're implying security is an issue."

"Not really. This is large place, and if you want to get in, you will. No different than living anywhere else."

"But you'd notice if someone didn't belong on the property?"

"Maybe. We have over six hundred residents, with scores of friends and family, and plenty of vendors and service personnel on the property."

Was she trying to depress me? "I understand that, but I'm sure, after dinner, it quiets down."

"Barring an evening event, and there's quite a few here, Palm Shores has a certain rhythm to it."

"Did you see who Mr. Coby's visitor was?"

"No. We sat together for dinner most evenings, and that night he said he was going to miss a screening of *A Star is Born* because he had to meet someone. It must have been important because he said on several occasions that he wanted to see the remake."

She was too much of a lady to pry into Coby's business. "Any idea on who it might have been?"

"I thought it might have something to do with his estate,

or something like that. People are particularly private about subjects like that."

"Did he ever mention any concerns about the inheritance he would leave?"

"No, but financial matters are rarely discussed among residents."

"Who was he close to?"

"I believe he and Mark Banner were probably the closest. And like everyone, he seemed to enjoy talking to Ben Porter. The man is always kidding around."

"Anyone else?"

"No. Bill wasn't here that long . . ."

"Did you notice any change in his behavior since he'd been here?"

"Nothing noticeable."

"So, the last time you saw Mr. Coby was at dinner?"

"Close up, yes. I saw him talking to Ben Porter when I went for a walk before the movie came on."

"Where were they?"

"By the entrance to Bill's building."

18

Sitting in a far corner of Palm Shore's gathering space. I watched Ryan Hall flirt with a group of women playing Scrabble. I wondered whether he truly enjoyed playing the game or if he was making an investment in getting referrals when my appointment entered.

The blue scrub top that Galena Vuvich wore couldn't conceal the muffin top bulging over the top of her pants. The aide didn't bend down when giving a kiss to a resident doing a jigsaw puzzle at a nearby table.

The five-inch Orthodox cross around her neck swayed as she headed toward me. Her crepe-soled shoes squeaked as she extended her hand. "Galena Vuvich. Nice to meet you."

Her handshake was firm and determined, matching the look on her face. "Thank you for taking the time to talk."

She sat, the tips of her shoes grazing the floor. "You want to know about Bill Coby?"

"Yes. How well did you know him?"

"He was a good man. Always with smile. He will be with God."

"You got along with him?"

"Galena get along with everybody."

Did she just refer to herself in the third person? "I understand you're on the property often."

"Most times, Galena work seven days, each week."

"You probably know a lot about Palm Shores, its residents, and the people who work here."

"Not a lot—everything. Galena's number one job is to take care of Miss Martha, but Galena keeps her eyes open."

"Do you have any idea who could have done this to Mr. Coby?"

"Many people; they have the fake faces. They make nice when the family is here, but when no one is looking, they change to evil."

I lost my father too early, but I could still hear him tell me that a real man did the right thing, even when no one was looking. "Do you have anyone in particular?"

"The nurse is very nasty woman. And that Porter, the maintenance man, he is always with the smile, but he is into the voodoo."

Voodoo? It felt like it was time to wrap this up. "I appreciate your honesty. Let me ask you about the people who manage or own Palm Shores—"

She rubbed her forefinger against a thumb. "It is business to them. They want the money."

"Can you give me an example?"

"Too many interns. They don't have to pay them."

"I'm sure they're not in critical roles."

"Everything is critical. I know many people don't like to say they are aide. But Galena know this is important position."

"No doubt. You have to be a special person to do what you do."

When she smiled, the gap between her teeth seemed to widen.

"Is there anything else you'd describe as cutting corners to save money?"

"The kitchen. I get snack for my lady, and they use the leftover foods, sometimes for two days."

So, it was stale bread and teenagers on their way to a nursing degree that I got for half an hour of my time. "You've been very helpful. I've got to get going."

She slid out of her chair, grabbed my wrist, and whispered, "Galena says to watch Mr. Morley and maintenance man."

"Excuse me?"

"Why are boss and fix-it man always talking? Always whispering?"

Was she off her rocker or pretending to be nuts so I'd leave her alone?

———

HALFWAY DOWN TRADE CENTER WAY, the Visual Universe was sandwiched between Sweet Art Gallery and Donnie's Framing. The gray building was dated and better suited to housing repair shops for vacuums and typewriters.

I pushed through the glass door into a small room whose walls were covered with paintings. A voice from the back said he'd be with me in a minute. I was taking a long look at a piece called "Blue Mystery," trying to figure out what made it worth twelve hundred, when Robard entered.

He was wiping his hands on a paint-splashed apron and had a smudge of yellow paint on his forehead.

"That's one of my personal favorites. It took me longer

than usual. Each time I added a layer of paint, it called for another."

I wanted to ask him if the amount of paint used increased the price. "It's interesting. You've been an artist your whole life?"

"Oh yeah. Ever since I can remember, I've been drawing and painting. Going to museums. It's like, I don't want to paint, I have to."

Was it the fact that he had a brush with the law that made him appear shifty? "Good way to put it. You self-taught, or did you go to school?"

"I was an art major but dropped out. I wanted to focus on contemporary art, and they wouldn't permit it. So, I left."

When I nodded, he pointed at the blue painting. "There's a little room in the price, if you're serious."

"I didn't come in for art." I handed him my card.

Robard didn't flinch. "What can I help you with, then?"

"Santa Monica."

"What's that supposed to mean?"

His soul patch had begun to gray. "You got yourself into trouble there."

"I had nothing to do with that, and if you don't know already, the charges were dropped. I got caught up in what those guys were doing."

"You know what I find interesting? How you couldn't know the pieces you were selling weren't originals."

"I just didn't. Nobody knows who did every painting that was ever made."

"True, but according to every gallery owner I've spoken to, it's a central part of their job to know the . . . what do they call it . . . the provenance of what they're selling."

"Look, that was a long time ago, and all I did was let these guys hang some pieces in my store."

"How'd you get compensated for letting them use your space?"

"When a piece sold, I took my commission."

"How much?"

"Twenty percent."

"That's cheap. According to the record, your so-called suppliers weren't the business type. You could have charged them a lot more."

"It wouldn't be fair to take advantage and charge them more than the going rate."

"Why didn't any of the buyers press charges? They had a legal right to make a claim against you and your gallery."

"Why don't you go ask them?"

"You know what I think? I believe you told them they were originals and stolen. They jumped at the chance to buy them at a large discount."

"Not true, man. You got it wrong."

"Maybe. You running the same scheme down here?"

"Scheme? What are you talking about? You're crazy, man. I'm done talking. Please leave the premises."

19

MAKING A RIGHT ONTO AIRPORT PULLING ROAD, I TRIED TO evaluate my encounter. Robard had a different air about him, and it wasn't the artist in him. The feeling I was getting was familiar. The criminal factor gnawed at me. Something was there.

Try as I could, I couldn't peel away enough layers from the internal messaging I was getting about Robard. My instincts were better suited to getting inside the mind of a killer. The painter was shady at best but not a life taker, and creative types think differently.

What was Robard up to, and how was it related to the burglary gang? He was experienced running scams pushing replicated artwork as originals. Those were outright sales. The crew breaking and entering homes were taking stuff out.

Pulling into the municipal complex, I wondered if it was possible that Robard had somehow identified valuable pieces he could steal and resell?

If that were the case, why hadn't any of the homeowners complained that they had lost a precious painting? It made no sense. Unless. Could the artwork have been stolen twice?

A horn beeped behind me. I took my foot off the brake, passed through a stop sign, and made a right into my building's lot.

Parking in a space, I sat there. It seemed impossible, but most homeowners had said they bought art from Visual Universe. Had he sold them paintings that had been stolen, then broke in and stolen them back?

The probability he had brought his scam show to Naples pulsated like the start of a toothache. Figuring that he had, I wondered why he'd skipped some sort of reenactment in Chitown? The weather would motivate most people to flee, but why not depart after pulling a scam?

My phone rang. It was Bilotti.

"Hey, Doc. How are you?"

"Good. You have a minute?"

By the tone of his voice, I knew he wasn't calling with a wine recommendation. "Sure. I'm in the car."

"I reviewed the autopsy report on Charles Martin, and it's disturbing."

"Are you telling me what I think you are?"

"Mr. Martin had a significant amount of Rohypnol in his body. More than enough to cause death."

"Are you sure?"

"Considering the circumstances surrounding the Coby death, I'd say it appears we have a serial killer on our hands."

"This may be the biggest case we've ever had."

"It's unimaginable. A psychopath is apparently targeting the elderly."

"This is right behind pedophilia."

"Twisted as it is, with mercy killings, at least there's a goal to relieve suffering. These two were healthy. What could be the motivation?"

"Greed."

"If it's inheritance, you should be able to find the link between the two easily."

"What do you think about the possibility that the people who own Palm Shores are killing off its residents?"

"Uh, that doesn't make sense. It would be like shooting themselves in the foot. They're getting paid every month."

"On the surface, it appears self-destructive. But this place has a different business model. Some people hand over a chunk of dough when they move in to get lower monthly fees."

"So, they get lower fees in exchange for the use of their money. Like a mortgage, to save on interest."

"Not exactly, but the main difference here is when they move out or die, they don't get it all back."

"They forfeit a portion? Who would agree to that?"

"It's like a reverse annuity, I guess. Hand over what you have, and instead of a predictable stream of income, they get lower costs. Everybody, especially the elderly, is worried their money is going to run out. With something like this, they'd get assurance their money would last long enough."

"I don't know, Frank. It's essentially a bet on how long they'll live."

It certainly was. But what they didn't figure was the possibility that the house was rigging the system. "They make it pretty compelling to hand over a chunk of money. We did some checking, and depending on the unit, you only need to live four years to break even."

"It's difficult for a healthy individual to believe they're not going to be alive in four years. But getting a senior to part with a significant sum of money isn't easy either."

That was true, but Bilotti hadn't seen the place nor been charmed by their marketing pro. "Age isn't always a factor, Doc. You'd need a gun to get me to write the check."

"Me too. You really think there's a greed-driven conspiracy?"

"I can't discount it. It's early, and we have several angles to pursue."

"I've been reading a bit about the coming divide between the old and the young. There's a movement beginning where the young believe that seniors are soaking up too many of the country's resources. They claim too much money is going to entitlements, and there won't be enough for their generation."

"Entitlements? Last time I looked, I'm paying into Social Security. It's our money."

"Agreed."

"What do they want to do, kill anyone over fifty?"

"If you find any sympathizers during the investigation, you may want to take a closer look at them."

"That'd be something like financial euthanasia. Not the so-called quality of life someone has but their standard of living."

"Good way to think of it."

"If it comes to that, I'm going to move the family to Italy and work in a Tuscan winery. At least we'd eat and drink well."

"Sounds like a plan. We may come along."

AFTER EVERY GOOGLE SEARCH, where I looked for any info on theft or fraud in Chicago's art world, I'd check my phone. Mary Ann was at the neurologist's office. Her primary doctor checked her out and wasn't concerned. He suggested it might be her schedule and age but recommended she see a specialist.

Mary Ann didn't want to go to another doctor and was

comfortable with the clearance her primary had given her. But after what I had gone through with the shifting diagnosis of my cancer, I pushed Mary Ann to make an appointment. She did but insisted on going alone and not making a big deal of it.

I was reading a small piece in the *Chicago Tribune*. It concerned a theft from a small gallery where the thieves had disabled the alarm system. My cell vibrated. It was Mary Ann.

"What did the doctor say?"

The crack in her voice told me all I needed to know.

20

─────────

I PEELED THE STICKY NOTE OFF THE SEAT OF MY CHAIR. Derrick had written the number for Dylan Nealy, the friend who gave me a primer on the assisted living business. He had called twice. It was only eleven thirty. Dialing the number, I wondered what was so damn urgent? Health issues like Mary Ann's were pressing, not blowing some incident out of proportion.

"Dylan Nealy."

"Hey, Dylan, it's Frank Luca. What's going on?"

"I'm sorry to call twice, but I thought you should know something."

"Go ahead."

"It's not public, but the news is Palm Shores is up for sale."

"They're selling?"

"That's what it looks like. They've been talking to Spring Point, a large Presbyterian outfit looking to expand in the South."

"Any idea on what a place like that would go for?"

"Deals in our space go at a multiple of earnings. If you

make a million dollars, you'll get six or seven million, depending on the size of the place."

"How much you think Palm Shores makes a year?"

"It's tough to say. They have high prices, but it isn't cheap to deliver what they do."

"Why do you think they're getting out?"

"The market is hot right now. Look at the demographics of the country. It's a space that's growing, and there's plenty of money up for grabs."

"Get out while the going's good?"

"Could be, or your investigation has them scared."

"You think there may be a bidding war to buy them?"

"I'm sure somebody else is going to jump in when word gets around. Then the multiple may get to nine or ten times what they earn."

"I'd appreciate you keeping me updated as this develops."

Sitting back in my chair, I rolled around what I'd learned. Was this connected to the case? I considered the possible sales price and the age of the owners. Was it simply an opportunity to take advantage of the hot market for senior housing?

My pee-pee alarm sounded, and I went to the bathroom to relieve the bladder doctors had made to replace my cancer-ridden one. As I pushed through the men's room door, the realization that the owners of Palm Shores had a huge financial incentive to boost earnings hit me.

It was more than the hundred and fifty thousand they kept from Bill Coby and Charles Martin. That hundred and a half, times the ten multiple they'd get by selling, was over a million and a half dollars.

That was more than enough money for a motive, and who knew if there were others who had checked out of Palm Shores earlier than they should have? I resolved to check on all deaths that occurred there over a three-year period.

Washing up, I hoped we wouldn't uncover a scheme that had been running for years. Any kind of conspiracy would make national news and be all over the TV. It would be another impossible thing to explain to Jessie. Thinking of our daughter, my mind yanked back to my wife.

The doctor advised Mary Ann not to search the internet for information. It was sound counsel but impossible to follow. As soon as I got back to my desk, I started asking Dr. Google for answers.

There was a ton of information, and I gravitated to an entry from the Mayo Clinic. It was too early in the game for her case, but what I was reading when Derrick came in was not encouraging.

I looked up, averting my eyes, and he said, "What's the matter?"

Shaking my head, I had to fight off the urge to cry. It was one of the weirdest feelings I ever had. I shrugged instead.

He sat on the edge of my desk. "Come on, man. What's going on?"

"Mary Ann has MS."

"Multiple sclerosis?"

I nodded.

"Damn. I know it's scary, man, but they got all kinds of treatments these days. A friend of my aunt has had it for twenty years, and you can hardly tell."

"She's lucky, then. We don't know yet if Mary Ann's is going to get much worse or be a mild case."

I blinked away a tear when he put his hand on my shoulder. "I'm sure she's going to be all right."

"I hope so. My whole world feels like it's coming down on me. How's Jessie going to deal with all this?"

"No matter what comes your way, you'll handle it. It's a tough challenge, but you'll get through it. You're the strongest man I know, and I'm going to be there with you every step of the way."

"I don't know about that."

"Well, I do. What's next?"

"She needs to get some kind of an electrical nerve test and another MRI to get a better idea of what's going on."

"When's that going to happen?"

"Next week."

"You want to take off the rest of the afternoon?"

"No way. I need to keep my mind engaged or I'll go crazy."

"Come on, let's go see the other Coby son. I'll drive."

"Okay, it'll keep me off the internet."

Interviewing Coby's younger son was something I'd asked Derrick to do, and now I felt bad about it. I gave him the assignment because after getting background information from Ronnie, I didn't think there was anything to him. I didn't want to waste my time, but he still had to be checked out.

How could I have treated Derrick that way? He was not only a good cop, but he had just proved how much he cared about me. Life seemed to work that way for me. Anytime I didn't do the right thing by someone, the next moment, they'd lift me onto a pedestal.

MY MIND DRIFTED during the interview. I let Derrick handle most of the questioning. It became fairly evident that pursuing the younger Coby son over killing his dad for money was a dead end. There didn't seem to be an easy answer to who had murdered two at Palm Shores.

This case would take time and require focus. Mustering

both looked to be a problem for me. Who knew what direction Mary Ann's condition would push us? A treadmill of doctor visits and tests? Would her physical condition quickly deteriorate, necessitating a total makeover of our lives? Or would she be one of the fortunate victims with a slowly progressing disease that required accommodations but not drastic changes to her life?

21

Derrick had several documents spread over his desk, but what caught my attention was the cup of Starbucks on my desk.

"Morning, Derrick."

"Morning. How's everything at home?"

"It's okay. We're waiting to take the tests."

"That's the hardest part."

"Tell me about it. What do you have there?"

"The death records for the last year."

"And?"

"They look legit. There's not an unnatural death on any of the death certificates. More than half are from cancer, the rest are heart attacks, and three people were over a hundred."

"Heart attacks? That could be bullshit."

"I don't think so. Every one of them had heart disease for years."

"Phew. I was afraid we'd be looking at something even worse than what we have."

"Me too. I was talking to Lynn about it last night. I don't

know, maybe it's because we're going to have a kid, but this case is getting to me."

Was he morphing into a copy of me? "You got to be careful not to let it get to you, or we won't be able to do the job."

"I know, but if someone is killing seniors for money or whatever, what does this say about the world we live in?"

"I wish I had the answer, partner. But it's up to us to get as many of these deviants off the streets as we can." We had to do that, but what I didn't know was whether it would make a difference in the world our kids would inherit.

Derrick came over and sat in the chair in front of my desk. He lowered his voice. "Do you ever feel like, what's the point of what we do? I mean, I know we have to nail people who kill, but it just feels like a losing cause."

We were partners and had become good friends, but I couldn't say what I wanted to. Some thoughts and feelings are best kept to yourself. We're human, and we have some dark and crazy things roaming between our ears. Being brutally honest and letting them out would alter opinions and outlooks.

"It's natural to get down, buddy. It happens from time to time, but I just shake it off, telling myself how much worse it would be. You came out of DC; you should know."

"Yeah, but we're just cleaning up, catching who did it. We need to stop it before it happens, and the bottom line is, we're not."

"That's not entirely true. We can and do change behavior. By bringing these bastards to justice, we're dissuading others from committing crimes. Plus we're giving law-abiding citizens confidence in the system."

"We threw a ton of criminals behind bars, but it didn't

stop anyone up in DC. The gangs grew in size and strength anyway."

"Washington might be a lost cause, but Collier County is home and it's damn safe. I'll tell you right now, I'll die trying to keep it that way."

WAITING TO SPEAK WITH MORLEY, I watched a woman being pushed in a wheelchair. Was that going to be Mary Ann in a year or two? I knew it was immature to feel it was unfair, but what bothered me wasn't what might happen to Mary Ann. Rattling in my head was the effect this would have on Jessie.

Kids are more adaptable than we think, but I wanted her to have a normal childhood. A mother she could run around with. I didn't want her life to be limited because she'd feel obligated to take care of her mom. It was my job to step up, if and whenever necessary, signaling that she didn't have to be preoccupied with her mother.

"Detective Luca, welcome again to Palm Shores."

Fred Morley was wearing another double-breasted jacket, but this time he had a paisley handkerchief sticking out of a pocket. His handshake was firmer. He was signaling confidence.

Morley praised the low humidity as we went to his office. He swept a notebook off his desk, shoving it into a drawer as he sat down. "How can we help you?"

"You've tightened security."

"Yes, we've added three guards to assure residents they're not in any danger."

I didn't think a visual force would calm anyone down. "It's early, but we're of the opinion it's an inside job."

He cocked his head. "Someone who works here?"

"A person or persons with full access."

"That's difficult to believe. Everyone in the Palm Shores family is dedicated to our residents."

"This is no time for naïvety, Mr. Morley. Everyone on the property is a potential suspect."

He smiled. "Well, you can save your time looking at me." He picked something off his desk. "Oh, here's the video of the building Mr. Coby lived in."

I pocketed the flash drive and asked, "Why didn't you tell me Palm Shores is up for sale?"

"There was no reason to. We're a private business, and it's unrelated to the unfortunate events that occurred."

I thought I'd heard every way to describe a homicide, but "event" was a new one. "Let me remind you that the murders occurred on your property, under your care, and supervision. From this moment on, anyone or anything concerning Palm Shores is related to the investigation I'm conducting. Is that clear?"

"Uh, yes. Of course. I hope you understand I wasn't attempting to prevent or deny access. You have free rein. I would just ask, if you can, that you try to keep things on an even keel. We don't want to alarm our residents."

"What percentage of your residents have chosen to buy down their monthly fees by handing over large sums of money?"

"Forgive me, Detective, but they're not handing over their money, they're opting for lower fees. It's tantamount to prepaying a portion of the fees in the years ahead."

"What's the percentage?"

"It's low, maybe twenty percent or so. People have an aversion to parting with their life savings."

"Just twenty percent, yet the two murdered men were both in that group."

"Really? I wasn't aware of that."

"As a result of their deaths, both men forfeited substantial sums, and you're telling me, as the managing partner, you didn't know about that?"

"I, I don't keep track of such things. My responsibilities are wide ranging. I'm pulled in so many directions here; it's not an easy job."

"You're an owner, and as such, benefited from both deaths."

"You think I did it? Come on. You really can't suspect me of this, do you?"

"Financial gain is a powerful motive, Mr. Morley."

"I don't mean to offend you, Detective, but that's ridiculous. I've dedicated my life to providing the highest quality life experience possible for seniors. It's my life's work and one I wouldn't jeopardize for a few dollars."

It was a sound defense, but we weren't talking about a paltry sum of money. I didn't want to hit him too hard at this time. "That's understandable, and you have built quite a place here."

The tension left his face. "Thank you. We're proud of what we've accomplished."

"Who would you suspect is responsible for these deaths?"

"I don't consider myself ignorant, but I cannot think of anyone on my own."

"On your own?"

"Since these events, a few of our residents have come to me, making accusations against a couple of individuals. There's nothing concrete about them, otherwise I would have come to you with them."

"Who are we talking about?"

"The residents mentioned our maintenance man, Ben Porter, and Galena Vuvich, a private aide."

Hearing those names again took my mind completely off Mary Ann and focused it on the case. This could be the break we needed to protect another senior from meeting the same fate as Coby and Martin.

22

———

I NEVER CAME HOME FOR LUNCH, BUT I THOUGHT MARY ANN could use the support and a surprise. She wasn't in the kitchen or on the lanai. I headed to the bedroom and heard Mary Ann shout, "Where the hell is it?"

The bedroom looked like it had been ransacked. Mary Ann was on her hands and knees in the closet.

"What's going on?"

"I can't find my earrings, the oval-shaped ones that Jessica likes."

"When did you wear them last?"

She started sobbing. "Why is everything happening to me?"

I sat on the floor and held her. "Take it easy. We'll find them."

"It's not the damn earrings: it's everything."

I knew everything meant MS and the uncertainty it had inserted into our lives. "I know it's tough, but let's wait till we have more info before we panic."

"I'm trying, but I'm, I'm too scared."

"That's normal, honey. I'm a little spooked about it myself."

"Do you think my case is going to be a bad one?"

"No. You're healthy and young."

"That don't mean anything. If it did, why'd I get it?"

"I wish I knew. But there are certain things in life that are just unknowable. That probably doesn't help, but it's true."

"I guess so."

"Come on, let's go to the lanai."

As soon as I slid open the door, I said, "There they are."

Her earrings were sitting on the table. Had I overlooked them when I searched for Mary Ann? Or was the universe cutting us a break?

BEN PORTER WORKED the two-to-ten shift, putting the maintenance man on the property when the lethal doses could have been delivered. When I returned to Palm Shores that afternoon, I found him waxing the floor of the beauty salon. He was singing as he worked, the ceiling's fluorescent light reflecting off his bald head.

"Got a minute, Mr. Porter?"

He turned around. His smile revealed a large gap between his front teeth. "Yes, sir." He shut the buffing machine off and moved it against the wall, dragging a yellow cone near it.

"I'm Detective Luca with the Collier Sheriff's Office."

"They told me you'd be coming around."

The forty-five-year-old had a slight Jamaican accent. "Said who?"

"Mrs. Brogan. She's Mr. Morley's secretary."

"You knew both Bill Coby and Charlie Martin."

"No more than anyone else."

"Really?"

"I get around this place. Some of the folks here are nice. They're bored though. We got a lot of things to do, but most of the people just ain't wanting to, you know, learn how to dance. You know what I mean? Talking is what they do to pass the time."

"Where were you May first, the night John Martin died?"

"Right here, working."

"Exactly where, from six to eight p.m.?"

"Oh, that's dinnertime, so I'm cleaning the kitchen prep areas. I do it each night. You know, we keep it clean here. Cleanliness is next to Godliness: Leviticus fifteen, not that I'm a Christian. My thing's voudon."

"Voudon? I'm sorry, I don't know what that is."

"It's an Afro-Caribbean religion. It started in Haiti and moved to my country, Jamaica."

My country? He was naturalized as an American citizen twenty years ago.

"The movies call it voodoo, to ruin the reputation. We are spiritual people, you know. We know spirits work with a God who wants to stop suffering and have us join him."

I had to ask, "Do you use those dolls?"

He smiled broadly. I caught a glimpse of a couple of gold fillings. "Only in Hollywood."

"A witness placed you with Mr. Coby in front of his building after dinner the night of his death."

He shook his head. "It wasn't me. They must be confusing me with somebody else."

People make mistakes in time and dates all the time. It's what makes eyewitnesses so unreliable. However, Lois Gershwin seemed as clear eyed and accurate as anyone I'd met. She could have been wrong, but I'd check the video.

"What do you know about Galena Vuvich?"

He smiled. "She don't like me, but it doesn't bother me none. The spirits tell us to act with kindness. It's the only way."

"Why do you say she doesn't like you?"

"It's not right to talk when she's not here."

"She's also religious?"

"Russian Orthodox. Maybe that's her reason. She says I practice voodoo." He laughed. "Many people are ignorant. They're living in denial. Denial we are one people; denial we will die; denial we must go to the Creator."

I wanted eternal life as much as the next guy, but with a double homicide to solve and Mary Ann's situation, I had more pressing problems to consider.

"Tell me about Charles Martin."

He shrugged. "Not much to say. I didn't know him other than to say hello."

Though a couple of people had said he knew both dead men, Porter was trying to tell me he hardly knew them. Why?

Making my way to the next appointment, I spied Hall slipping into the bathroom. It wasn't fair, but I followed him, curious if he was going to do a line of coke.

I opened the door slowly and slipped in. Hall was in a stall. I stood silently for a moment. When I heard him snorting, I cleared my throat and left.

MARK BANNER LIVED in the same building Bill Coby had. He was bent at the waist but had a head of black hair decorated by just a handful of gray hairs. I looked closely; it wasn't dyed.

The main room of his apartment gave me a touch of claustrophobia. A pair of sliders, leading to a bathtub-sized lanai, provided the only natural light. I was relieved when we sat by the doors rather than the kitchen counter.

"I understand you and Bill Coby were good friends."

"We hit it off as soon as he moved in. I miss him. He had so much energy, he pulled me along."

"When was the last time you saw him?"

"I had been out to dinner with my son Pauly. He takes me out once a week. We go to Jimmy P's Charred and have a big steak. I don't care what the doctors tell me about red meat. I love my steak. You like meat?"

"Occasionally. How is Jimmy P's? I heard a lot about it."

"Don't tell me you've never been."

I shook my head.

"Well, young man, it's fabulous. Get their Manhattan Cut steak. I promise you won't be disappointed."

It was the second time I'd been called young man. This place was starting to grow on me. "Where did you see Bill Coby?"

"When I came back from dinner. I saw him talking to Ben Porter. Bill always kidded me about the doggy bag I'd bring back for lunch the next day."

"And you're certain it was Ben Porter, the maintenance man, he was chatting with?"

"Absolutely. Ben even said if I didn't want to eat the leftovers for lunch that he'd take them."

"And you're sure it was the last night Bill Coby was alive?"

"Who could forget something like that? I remember that morning clear as a bell. I went to breakfast, and he wasn't there, but sometimes he'd skip and have coffee in his place. But when I came back, there were people hanging around out front. I knew something was up and asked. Bill was dead."

"Did he mention anything about a visitor he was expecting that night?"

"No. I don't know about that."

"Mr. Banner, do you know of anyone who might have done this?"

He shook his head. "I wish I did, but between going out a couple of days with my family and keeping to myself, I don't know all the inner workings, if you know what I mean."

"I understand."

"You know, you should ask the Russian lady. She's the unofficial mayor around here."

"Galena Vuvich?"

"Yeah, you can't miss her. She's built like a bowling ball and wears a big cross."

23

Publix was packed with after-work shoppers, including me. I grabbed the last item on my list, a box of Rice Chex, and rolled my cart to the checkout area. Line three was the shortest by far, and I slid in behind two other shoppers, wondering why the line wasn't packed like the others.

Laying a bottle of olive oil on the conveyor belt, I noticed a familiar face pushing a cart toward my line. It was Robert Crenshaw, the owner of the Longboat Drive house that'd been burglarized.

He pretended not to see me and veered toward a longer line.

"This is the shortest line, Mr. Crenshaw."

The color drained from his face. "Oh, thank you."

"We met at your home. I'm Detective Luca."

"Oh, I, yes. That's right."

People got nervous around cops, and also when you saw someone out of the context that you knew them from, but he was way too jittery. I'd seen this before, and it wasn't a class thing.

"How long you in town for?"

"We're leaving tomorrow."

I eyed his overflowing cart. He was hiding something. "Back to the real world?"

He nodded and began putting some items behind mine. I checked out and waited for him outside. A few minutes went by and he exited. Rolling over to him, I decided to take a shot. "A friend of yours said to say hello."

His eyes widened. "Who?"

"Pierre Robard."

He put both hands on his cart. "He's not a friend."

"Really? He said he'd given you a special discount on a painting."

"I, I have to go. My wife is waiting; she's not feeling well."

He pushed his cart like he was in a race to a Jaguar SUV. His wife might have been waiting, but not here.

DERRICK WAS REVIEWING video from Palm Shores, and I . . . well, I was trolling the internet for information on multiple sclerosis. I'd read more case studies than a premed student and felt as if I were standing on a wakeboard on a windy day.

The bottom line seemed to be that there was no way to predict how her disease would progress. Even with the tests she would soon take, the results would not indicate what life would be like. Some patients reacted favorably to the drugs used to treat the disease, and others saw little, if any, improvement.

Derrick said, "You all right, Frank?"

"Uh, yeah, sure. Why?"

"You're staring like a zombie."

"Guess I zoned out. I can't get to sleep; my mind's racing."

"That's understandable. Why don't you take something? Try a Unisom or a Tylenol PM."

"I don't want to get started with stuff like that."

"Maybe you should talk to someone."

Though I knew exactly what he meant, I said, "What do you mean?"

"The department has resources to help you process what your family is going through."

"Yeah, right. I go to see their shrink, and the next thing I know, they'll take me off the street and put me behind a desk."

"You think they'd do that?"

"In a heartbeat. I'm not saying they're totally wrong, but if they have the slightest inclination you're not fit for duty, they pull you inside."

"I get it, but that discourages people from getting help."

"Anybody who's been around a while would never go to someone internally."

The name Dr. Bruno pooped into my head. She had helped me get over my fears of becoming a father. Maybe I should schedule a chat with her.

"That's a shame."

"Sure is. Get back to the video. We need a break of some kind. I'm going to see Vuvich."

THE BACKGROUND on Galena Vuvich was sketchy at best. My request to the Ukrainian authorities only turned up a birth record. Nothing else. No baptismal certificate, driver's license, or education records. It was strange and concerning.

The possibility that she had somehow used a stolen identity when she emigrated was real. When the Soviet Union collapsed, anything, including identity papers, could be bought for a few dollars during the chaos. I'd submitted an inquiry to Interpol but wasn't expecting much. The records looked to have been whitewashed and the truth buried forever.

Galena was sitting at a table with a woman I assumed was her client. The dining room was full. It was a quarter to noon. I tried to catch her eye, but she shot out of her chair and headed toward a staffer.

Animated, the Ukrainian got in the worker's face. She said her piece, and as she returned to the table, saw me waving. Vuvich threw up a finger, whispered to her client, and strode over. She was wearing a pair of athletic pants whose seams could be heard groaning, a red shirt, but no smile.

"You're early."

"I can wait."

"No." She pointed to a bench just beyond a pair of sliders and led the way.

The small courtyard was shaded and the metal settee cool. Galena centered the ornate cross she wore and said, "Did you talk to Voodoo Man and Morley?"

"I'm unable to discuss ongoing investigations."

She snorted. "Galena give you gift and you ignore."

"That's an interesting cross."

"It was my nana's."

"Your grandmother?"

"Yes. She give to Galena on her dying bed. Poor lady suffered for years. Very difficult to watch. No one should be in such pain. Now, she is in arms of God."

"She passed away in the Ukraine?"

"Yes. Nineteen eighty-eight. Galena leave one year after."

"You're religious?"

She waved her arm. "This world is nothing. Galena wait for eternal life." She crossed herself, but in the backward fashion of Orthodox Christians, a method developed to differentiate the sects during the century-old breach between the Eastern and Western churches.

"You were baptized before you came to America?"

"Yes."

"But there's no record of it."

"Nothing works under communism."

"How about the cars there? Do they work?"

"We have old, big American cars. Galena drive Malibu there."

"I hear it's easy to get in trouble in a communist country."

She smiled. "Yes, very easy for authorities to make arrest."

"Why did you tell me to watch Ben Porter?"

She leaned in. "He is evil man. Galena see him drink blood one time."

"He drank blood? Whose?"

She shrugged and shook her head. "Voodoo people. They kill the animals for sacrifice. They say the spirits will give them money. Maybe it work. He has new car now."

"Have you seen him lose his temper?"

"Many times. He give the smile, but he is angry man."

Porter was climbing the suspect ladder two rungs at a time.

24

Derrick had identified a man in his thirties entering Bill Coby's building at 7:45 p.m. He had long hair, was wearing a backpack, and carrying a briefcase. The man wasn't an employee of Palm Shores, and no one could identify him as a supplier or a visitor.

Who was this guy, and what was he doing there at that time? Most of the residents were winding down at that hour. Was he the killer?

We needed help from the public in identifying him. I wanted pictures of him distributed to the media and went to the Community Engagement Department to organize it. Leaving with a promise they'd get it out immediately, I had a good feeling someone would tell us who he was.

I had twenty minutes to get to my next stop. Just making the appointment had a calming effect on me. I was hoping it was going to live up to my expectations.

As I drove down her street, my palms began to sweat. This was a stupid idea. She didn't have a magic wand, and the reality was she couldn't change anything. Before turning into her driveway, I considered taking off.

The smell of baked goods greeted me again. I didn't care that it was probably an air freshener; it was nice. The door to her office was open. She smiled and waved me in.

"Good to see you, Mr. Luca."

"How are you, Dr. Bruno?"

"I'm fine. The question is, how are you?"

"I'm doing good."

"Let's sit over there."

We sat across from each other in the same gray chairs we'd used before. I declined a beverage offer and she asked, "What's on your mind, Frank?"

"I don't know what I'm going to do. Mary Ann has been diagnosed with MS."

"I'm sorry to hear that. What is the prognosis?"

"We're not sure yet. They need more testing to get an idea if it's severe or not."

"I wish her the best with it. Tell me how you feel about it."

"Terrible. I'm all mixed up. Jessie's only six, and I'm not equipped to deal with all of this. I'm scared. And pissed. Why is this happening to us?"

"It's completely normal to feel the way you do. Your concern is rooted in the love for her and your family. Try to explain what you're feeling."

"That I'm helpless. That I can't do anything to change things. It makes me crazy."

"You're frustrated because you feel your role is to protect your family, and in this case, you're unable to. That's a common reaction and completely normal. Let's examine that for a moment. Your wife's diagnosis is not a result of anything you did."

I nodded.

"You're not a neurologist, and even the experts in the field struggle with treatments for their patients."

I nodded again.

"The reality is, you have a right to be frustrated with the situation but not by your inability to impact the diagnosis. Does that make sense?"

"Yes. I see what you mean."

"Where you can have an impact is supporting your wife and daughter. How you handle changes that may occur and dealing with the stress that'll arise from the situations you may find yourselves in. That is something in your control."

"And it's not going to be easy."

"Of course not, but it is achievable. There are techniques to deploy that will help you manage your responses."

"What kinds of things are you talking about?"

"The most important point to remember is not to react immediately. To anything. You have to resist the urge to fly off the handle or say something that will hurt your wife or daughter."

"Think before I speak?"

"It should go a step beyond that. You can't control what happens, but you can control your response to it. Sometimes it's going to require you to fake it. You have to be positive even if the news or situation is bad."

"I understand that. I hope I'm up to it. What keeps me up nights is worrying about her and Jessie."

"Right now, it's all new and frightening. Once you have a clear diagnosis, some of the uncertainty will be removed."

"But if it's bad . . ."

"You have to be prepared for whatever comes. I realize how difficult this may become. You have a young daughter to take care of, and you may not get much help from your wife."

"It's a frigging nightmare."

"The first and most important thing to managing this is acceptance. You have to accept her condition and whatever effects it has on your family. Once you stop fighting and trying to change circumstances, you'll free yourself to deal with any changes."

"You want me to stop fighting? It's the only thing I know how to do."

"I'm not suggesting you give up. What I was referring to was the mental denial of her condition. This is the new reality for your family. Accept it, and you'll have the strength to pursue what needs to be done to keep life as normal as possible and to obtain the best treatments for her."

"What do I tell Jessie?"

"The truth. Don't sugarcoat it, and please don't lie to her. Children are stronger than you think, and there's no need to frame anything or shield her from what is going on."

"Tell here everything the doctors say?"

"Give her an accurate overview. When and if she asks questions, give her direct, truthful answers."

"I don't know. This is just screwed up."

"I don't believe I need to tell you that, one, you're not the only person confronting a situation like this, and two, though it's not good, it could be worse."

"I guess you're right."

"You know I am. You have to trade some of your expectations for some appreciation. Life is not going exactly how you may have planned it, but it's still good. If you concentrate on what you do have, instead of what could be, not only will you be happier, but it will make it easier to take care of your family."

It was good advice even though I didn't feel like I was a person who needed or expected much. I knew I had it good.

Beemers and Benzs didn't interest me. All I wanted was a normal family life, a happy child, and to catch bad guys.

Leaving Dr. Bruno's, I drove slowly, replaying what she had said. Bruno seemed to have a handle on how to live. Intellectually, I got it. The problem was implementing what she suggested. My priorities were Mary Ann and Jessie. Period. A distant second was the Palm Shore case.

I sped up and turned onto Airport Pulling Road when my cell rang.

"What's up, Derrick?"

"I dug into that gallery theft in Chicago, and guess what I found?"

Going only halfway to where Dr. Bruno suggested, I didn't get pissed about his guessing games, but said, "A Rembrandt for half off?"

"What?"

"Never mind. What did you learn?"

"One of the stolen pictures looks like it might be a match for one taken out of the Longboat Drive home."

"Tell me it's the one the Crenshaws left out when we asked for photos of the stolen artwork."

"Bingo."

"Get the lab to verify if they're one and the same."

25

Going to the public for help worked. The hotline received fifteen calls, all but one identified the man seen entering Bill Coby's building as Michael Finnery. He was a thirty-eight-year-old and managed the Timeless Eatery in the design district.

Finnery had been arrested when he was twenty-two on an assault charge that was dropped. He also lost his license at twenty-five for driving under the influence. They were yellow flags, but there had been nothing since then. Though I tried, I couldn't find a connection to Bill Coby.

I was out of ideas. So, even though it broke protocol, I ran the name by the murdered man's son. It was another dead end as Ronnie couldn't think of a link with his father. It was time to chat with Finnery. As I climbed into the Cherokee, a text from Derrick came in. Chester wanted an update.

The Timeless Eatery was fairly new. It was my first time there. I loved the rounded roof and glass front of the building it was in. The entrance was around the back, near a bar, open to the outside. Thirty-foot ceilings and a lack of walls made it feel larger than it was.

It was well before dinner, and the place was empty. I found Finnery near a brick pizza oven, writing the day's specials on a chalkboard.

"Mr. Finnery? I'm Detective Luca, with the Collier County Sheriff's Office."

"That's me. We violate some ordinance or something?"

He was relaxed. "I'd like to ask you a couple of questions. Can we talk here?"

"Sure, I'd love to get off my feet." He pointed to a couple of club chairs by a fireplace.

I settled into a chair and asked, "What were you doing at Palm Shores the night of May first?"

"Oh, this is about Bill, isn't it?"

"Yes. Why did you go to see him?"

"I was teaching him magic tricks."

"Magic tricks?"

"Yeah. I'm a magician. I work here to pay the bills."

"You went to show Bill Coby how to perform magic tricks the night he died?"

"Yep. Nothing fancy. He wanted to learn a couple of card tricks to show his grandkids. He used to fool around with cards when he was younger. He wanted to brush up, learn something new."

"Was that the first time you met with him?"

"Second. First one was about a month before."

"You teach others?"

He dug out a card. "Here's my card if you know anyone looking to learn."

I stared at the red business card that read: Card Trick Magic by Michael Finnery.

"How did you come to teach Mr. Coby?"

"He called me. I think somebody saw me do a show at Bayfront and told him to call. I'm there every other Sunday."

About to ask him to show me a trick I could show Jessie, I reconsidered. I'd broken enough protocols for the day. I wondered if what Dr. Bruno had said about not reacting was sinking in.

After finishing with Finnery, I walked into the sunshine. The heat felt good but wasn't enough to make up for the waste of time coming here. I was nowhere near solving the double homicide, and Chester wanted to see me.

CHESTER'S SLEEVES were rolled up. I don't know if he got some kind of deal on long-sleeved shirts, but that's all he wore. I understood during winter, when I wore undershirts, but wasn't it easier to wear short sleeves?

"Take a seat, Frank."

"Busy?"

"Always. How's everything at home?"

"Good."

"How is Mary Ann doing?"

"She's okay, sir. We're waiting to take a couple of tests to see what's going on."

"You need anything, you come to me. Understand?"

"Thank you, sir. We'll be fine."

"We have someone to talk with if you need."

"I know, but all is good."

"Let's hope it stays that way."

The amen was out of my mouth before I realized it.

"Indeed. Some weather we're having, huh?"

Maybe I was the same way, but Chester needed space between the personal and the police work. "It's been perfect. And with all the rain coming in the middle of the night, you can't ask for more."

"I hear a cold front is moving in."

"Like Einstein said, it's all relative."

"No truer words. Another example is the pressure I'm getting over the Palm Shores case. Between the seniors and the press, you'd think this place was the East Side of Chicago. I need this case solved, and quick."

"We're working a couple of promising angles."

"I'm surprised you haven't solved it yet. Is your situation at home interfering?"

I took a breath before answering. "Not at all."

"Then why don't we have a prime suspect yet?"

I shifted in my chair. The money paid to Dr. Bruno paying dividends. "It's not as easy as it may appear, sir."

"The murders occurred inside a gated facility, Luca. The victims' lives aren't complicated and are limited, in a large part, to Palm Shores. We're talking about men in their eighties, for God's sake."

"We have reason to believe it was someone working there."

"That's all you have?"

Rather than say yes, I said, "We're narrowing down the persons of interest."

"How soon until you have a prime?"

"It's tough to say, but we're going full speed on this."

"Do you want me to ask the Lee County sheriff to borrow a homicide detective?"

Instead of "how dare you," I said, "I don't believe that's necessary. Detective Dickson and I have this under control."

"Don't let me down, Luca."

"Don't worry. We'll get the person responsible for this."

"All right, that's all I have."

Unable to tell him to go screw off, I left without telling him we were close to solving the burglary case. The lack of support bothered me. Chester paid lip service to my personal situation before jumping on me. I wondered, if we really needed something, would he be there for us?

I couldn't waste energy on it. It could have been Dr. Bruno, or maybe it was just the fact that Mary Ann's condition had sharpened what was important to me.

Like most people, I'd lost perspective as the time lengthened since my recovery from cancer. People resorted to their old ways, even after a scare like the one I had.

Mary Ann's diagnosis was a reminder, and it was working. I was annoyed by Chester's behavior, but I wasn't angry like I'd tended to be. In the past, I'd fume for days afterward. Like they say, something good always comes out of a bad situation. But why did it have to be so damn bad?

26

It was time to have another talk with Ben Porter. I wanted to bring him in, but getting a chance to see his place would give me a slice of insight I wouldn't otherwise get without a warrant.

I did a double take. His address was 100 Bayfront Place. This guy lived in Bayfront? Pulling up Zillow, I plugged in his unit number. The estimated value was eight hundred thousand. His salary as a maintenance man could never support this place. Most people would choke on the maintenance fees alone.

Checking the tax records, I found out he'd only owned it for a month. Interestingly, there didn't appear to be a mortgage on the condo either.

Was Porter somehow profiting from the murders? Was he working with someone like Morley, who was paying him to kill? What Galena said the first time about the two of them rang in my ears.

Rather than claiming another Olympic medal in jumping to conclusions, I tried dismantling the nascent theory. How would Morley even approach someone like Porter? Money is a powerful motivator, but there are a limited number of men willing to do contract killings.

Conspiracies aren't something I generally believe in. This one was unlikely, but I couldn't jettison the idea. I called Porter to let him know I was coming. There was no answer. I left a voice mail telling him I'd be there at ten the next morning.

MARY ANN and I were sitting in a stark-white waiting room, talking about Jessie and the upcoming school year. I was reiterating my refusal to get a cell phone for our daughter when Mary Ann's name was called out.

Next thing I know, we're sitting in the doctor's office about to get the results from the tests she underwent. I grabbed Mary Ann's hand and kissed her cheek. My stomach felt like we were about to jump off a cliff.

Dr. Alessi swept into the office, asking Mary Ann how she felt as he plopped into his chair.

"I'm feeling pretty good. A little tired at times, but I feel good."

A little tired? She's been conking out at eight, nine, maximum, every night. Why do we tend to put a positive spin on our communications with a doctor? It's not going to change the diagnosis.

"Good. Shall we discuss your test results?"

Since no wasn't an option, we said yes in stereo.

"MS is a particularly difficult diagnosis to make, but between the MRI, the lumbar puncture, and the nerve speed test, I'm confident you have relapsing-remitting MS."

"What does that mean? Is she going to live a normal life?"

He smiled. "It's a mouthful. First of all, and it does vary, most people with this type of MS experience new symptoms or relapses over several days that usually go away completely. These relapses are usually followed by quiet periods where the disease goes into remission for months or even years at a time."

That seemed positive, but he never answered the question about a normal life. Mary Ann said, "That sounds promising."

"It is. Now, on the downside, about sixty to seventy percent of people with this type eventually decline, experiencing more symptoms and shorter periods or remissions, if any at all."

I squeezed her hand and asked, "How long until something like that?"

"It's impossible to say. Each case is entirely different."

"Is it a year or ten years?"

"I don't believe she'll experience any major lifestyle changes in the foreseeable future." While I was trying to put a number of years on what that meant, I heard him say, "Fortunately, your type of MS has a couple of treatment options available. They're not cures but can usually push against symptoms, slowing the progression of the disease, making day-to-day life easier."

I perked up. Everything was really going to be okay. Then he said, "However, I have to caution you. These treatments carry significant health risks, and as such, may be dangerous."

Dangerous was the last word I remember clearly. The rest of the time the doctor seemed to be speaking in a slow-motion jumble of words. I felt like I was watching it from above, a spectator rather than a participant. It was the same thing that happened when the doctor explained the severity of my bladder cancer.

I didn't return to reality until I heard Mary Ann ask about her life expectancy. All the time my focus had been on the possible physical challenges coming her way. I never thought she'd die from it.

Dr. Alessi said, "Life expectancy varies from patient to patient. You're in good overall health, which will help offset some negatives associated with the disease. The other factors are the extent of any treatment's effectiveness and the intensity of attacks and symptoms. Importantly, we also discovered that a patient's stress level has a direct impact on longevity."

That was it. Mary Ann was not going to be working any longer. We'd have to remove as much stress as possible. Having the sickness alone was more than enough stress for anyone.

As soon as we got outside, I hugged Mary Ann. I refrained from crying only because I heard Dr. Bruno whispering in my ear. Instead, I said, "Everything is going to be all right."

"You think so?"

"Absolutely. He said there are treatments that will help."

"But he said they were dangerous."

"They have to say that. It's like the warnings for all medicines. If you read the side effects for aspirin, you wouldn't take them."

"I guess."

"Don't worry. You're in good hands. I really like this doctor." I didn't know where all the optimism was coming from.

"He was more direct than I expected."

"That's the only way to be. Did you hear what he said about stress?"

"I know. It's bad for you in any case, but now . . ."

"You're retiring, my dear."

"What? Hold on a minute. I'll figure something out."

"Look, we can't fool around with this."

"I know, but . . ."

"How about you take a leave of absence; you spend more time with Jessie. See how it goes. If you feel good and want to, you go back."

"Let me think about it."

"Sure."

I knew she'd agree, but making such a big change in her day to day life would be an admission that MS had scored a victory. She had to let it sink in and make it look like it was her decision. It was the way I also worked.

The larger question was not whether she worked or not but what life would look like in a couple of years. Every semblance of the map of our future had been kicked into the unknown.

27

WE HAD AN EARLY DINNER. IT WAS ABOUT AS PHONY AS YOU can get. Maybe to an outsider it appeared that all was normal, but it was robotic. Jessie would have seen through it if she wasn't excited to be going to a neighbor's house for a party where women gather to buy costume jewelry.

The timing couldn't have been better. I dreaded trying to talk about the weather while a tornado was minutes away. I retreated to the lanai as my girls got ready. It was time to try and process this mess. I backed up to the scene where the doctor delivered the news.

Mary Ann had MS. Hearing that was even more dizzying than when the doctor told me I had cancer. Was it my love for her? Was it the frightening thought of being the main one responsible for Jessie? Or was it that my family was being threatened by an unseen enemy? A sneaky, formidable foe that I was powerless to combat.

I didn't know what to think or do. My life was being thrown upside down, and I didn't like it. Anger percolated in me. Was the origin of it my tendency to be selfish or my dire helplessness?

It wasn't a perfect life, but it was a damn good one. I had an amazing daughter, a fantastic wife as a partner, and a job that satisfied my need to hunt down killers. If that wasn't enough, we were happily living in a place I considered paradise.

But there were too many unknowns. I wanted answers. Why was this happening to me? To us? And what exactly was happening? I reached for my cell and made a call. I pecked both girls' cheeks and jumped into the Cherokee.

Driving south on Crayton Road, I made a left onto Turtle Hatch Road. I always liked Park Shore, but the lots were too small and the prices too high. Bilotti's house was twenty-five years old and ornamented with a good dose of stone castings. It wasn't a look I liked anymore, but well maintained was an understatement. Even in the fading light, the place looked like it had just been waxed.

I hit the bell and wasn't disappointed. The deep clang brought to mind Notre Dame, the cathedral in Paris, not the college. The destruction a recent fire had wrought snuck into my head but vanished when Bilotti opened the door.

"Come on in, Frank."

"Thanks, Doc. I'm sorry to barge in out of the blue—"

"Stop it right there. I'm glad you called."

"You sure I'm not interrupting anything?"

"Diane is volunteering at St. Matthew's House. I opened a nice Napa cabernet after you called. Sit down; I'll get the vino."

I sat in a brown tweed club chair and stared at the family picture on the coffee table. Bilotti and his wife were on either side of their two daughters, who were now in their midtwenties. They were perched over a vineyard that might have been in Europe. I knew nobody's life was perfect, but I'd be lying if I didn't say their bright, healthy smiles brought on a twinge of envy.

The doctor was not only ten years older than me but had his children earlier in life than I did. If it hadn't taken me so long to get my life together, Jessie would be older, and Mary Ann's condition would be less scary.

Bilotti set down his glass and poured one for me. "Let me know what you think of it."

I wanted to gulp it down but remembered to check the color and take a deep sniff before sipping it. "That's nice. What is it?"

"Morlet Family Vineyards. It's not as bold as most Napa cabs are. It's restrained, elegant."

I took another sip. "What am I tasting? Is it blackberries?"

"Very good. Try to taste the black currant and licorice overtones."

I didn't even know what black currant was, but I got the licorice. "I like it. It doesn't taste like a Napa cab though."

"The winemaker, Luke Morlet, was born in France. In fact, his family still makes champagne there."

"Expensive?"

He shrugged. "Nothing is too good for my favorite detective."

I raised my glass. "If you can't afford the best, it's good to have friends who can."

He clinked my glass. "The whole thing about wine is about sharing. It's like life: it's better with friends."

I was afraid I'd cry and took a sip.

"If you want to talk about anything, I'm here. If you just want to drink some wine together, you know I'm good with that. Okay?"

"Thanks." I took another sip to buy me a couple of seconds. "As a doctor, what can you tell me about MS?"

He launched into a technical explanation, and I cut him off. "I know all that medical stuff. Tell me what I can expect. What's going to happen to her?"

"Frank, you're a detective, and you want answers. I understand that. But what you're dealing with here is different. I know you don't want to hear it, but the bottom line is no one knows if and how her MS will progress."

He was right. I had come for answers. I needed to know what my future, our future, looked like. "What's a likely scenario?"

"I'm not a neurologist and haven't reviewed—"

"As a friend, not a doctor."

He took a sip of wine and set the glass down. "I believe you should be prepared for the worst. That's not to say it will happen, but it's the way to deal with it in the long term and also the flare-ups she'll experience from time to time."

Reassurance and comfort were what I came for. I was ready to bolt. "Why is this shit happening to us?"

"Nobody gets out of this world without getting crapped on."

"What? Getting bladder cancer wasn't enough? How much can anyone take?"

"I know it seems unfair, but thank God you beat the cancer."

"Believe me, Doc, I'm not ungrateful, but something like this? After what I went through?"

"The bigger the circle, the more likely something is going to happen."

"I don't get it."

"When you came down here, you were like a shark, not in a bad way, but you were a loner. You did your job but kept to yourself. Even today, you don't let people get too close. Am I right?"

I shrugged. I had to protect myself. Didn't I?

"Now you have a beautiful family, and it's a stab in the heart whenever anything bad happens to them. Especially when you're used to only worrying about yourself."

What did he know? I was the one who had cancer, and it was my wife with MS. "That's bullshit. It's not fair."

"As anyone over ten knows, life isn't fair. Stuff happens all the time to good people. You have a choice. Deal with it as best you can, or become angry and resentful. Believe me, when Debbie was diagnosed with leukemia at just six years old, I felt like we'd been run over by a cement truck. I couldn't do anything. Then I started lashing out, and you know what? It made things worse. Thank God I realized it before it was too late."

"Debbie had leukemia as a kid? You never said anything."

"I don't care what or who you are, everybody has their troubles and sicknesses to deal with. No sense dwelling on it."

"I know, but if something happened to Jessie, I don't know what I'd do."

"You'd deal with it. The best thing you can do right now is maintain a sense of normalcy. That's what Mary Ann and Jessica need. I don't mean to go into denial about it, it's a serious illness, but you're going to learn to live with it. Adjustments may be needed, but if you have the correct attitude, not only will your family benefit, but you will too. And all of you will be closer and stronger as a result."

The vino was good. The advice was sound, but implementing it was going to be a challenge.

28

———

By the lack of parking spaces, Bayfront looked like it had finally regained its footing. The multiuse development on the water had opened just as the real estate market began tumbling. It was a classic example of timing being everything.

Approaching Porter's building, I saw him sitting at an outdoor table at EJ's Bayfront Café. He was sipping a coffee and chatting with a kid in a Yankees hat at the next table. He gave me a wide smile and pointed to an empty chair.

"Have some coffee."

"No, thanks. Had two already."

He nodded.

"How long you been living in Bayfront?"

"A while."

Was he being sly, or had he rented beforehand? "You like it here?"

"It's not home. But the marina reminds me of Jamaica. There's a spiritualness around water."

Home again? He lived and worked in Florida but referred to Jamaica as home? "You have a boat?"

He hesitated before saying, "No. But I like to fish."

"I have a couple of questions for you."

He took a sip and shrugged.

"You sure you want to do this out here?"

He swiveled his head. "I'm at peace anywhere I am."

He was either denying me a chance to get intel from his condo or had nothing to fear. I looked into his eyes. The whites were tinged yellow, but I couldn't detect any more than the usual nervousness people have talking to the police.

"You told me you didn't know Bill Coby well."

"Uh-huh."

"You also told me that you weren't by his building the night he was last seen alive."

"I don't think I was."

"We have another witness who places you there, talking with Bill Coby after dinner."

"They could be wrong."

"They could. However, the video surveillance of the entrance confirms your presence there."

He shrugged. "Maybe I mixed the days up."

"You were speaking with Mr. Coby as well. What were you talking about?"

"I can't remember. If I did, I'd tell you."

"That's difficult to believe."

"You know how many people I talk to every day? And these people, they need to talk. Most are lonely."

Lonely? In a place with tons of people and activities? "Try to recall."

"I tried."

"Try harder."

"Sorry, man. I can't. It was probably nothing, like most of the talking. You know, how you doing? What you working on? The weather, that kind of thing. One thing about him, he had a sadness to him."

Coby had recently lost his wife. "How much do you earn at Palm Shores?"

"Sixteen fifty an hour."

"How'd you end up here?"

"My son, he does okay. He's a good boy."

It looked like he was getting help to elevate his lifestyle.

"That's nice of him. What's his name?"

"Francois."

The French had an outsized role in Jamaica, and it showed in the names. "This is expensive. You could get something cheaper and not have to work."

He smiled. "And do what? Sit around and watch TV?"

"You like to fish."

"Yeah, but not every day."

There was something. The problem was my inability to define what it was. He lied about being with Coby, and I wasn't buying a son who would buy him a million-dollar apartment but allow him to clean toilets.

"What does your son do?"

"He has a couple of business interests."

"Sounds like there's got to be a place for you to keep busy with him."

"Not good to mix business and family."

He was right, but I didn't buy it as an answer. I finished up with Porter, knowing it was time to go a couple of levels down.

DERRICK JUMPED out of his chair. "We got a tip while you were out."

"What's it about?"

"There's a visitor who goes to Palm Shores regularly. A guy named Brian Vape. Guess what he advocates?"

Here we go. Instead of telling him to get to the damn point, I hit him with, "Lower taxes?"

"Sorry."

"And? What about this Vape?"

"Apparently, he's all for euthanasia."

Sometimes I had to drag information out of Derrick like it was some kind of game. I loved the guy, but it took all I had to hold off exploding. "Tell me what you know."

"According to the caller, her mother lives in Palm Shores. This Vape guy is always complaining about the cost of taking care of the elderly and what a drain it is on the country's resources."

"So, we just kill them when they reach a certain age?"

"I read somewhere that Medicare, or maybe it was Medicaid, that twenty-five percent of all the money they spend is for caring for someone over sixty-five in the last year of their life."

"It's all about the quality of the last year. There's plenty of people being kept alive that have zero quality of life. But killing them off to save money? I'm not sure I want to live in a society like that. Who makes that call? One of the clowns in Washington?"

"I'm with you. It's a slippery slope. Next thing you know, kids with disabilities could be next."

"Heaven forbid. What else you have on this guy?"

"The caller said Vape visits his mother every evening. Most times he eats with her, but he comes every night."

"That fits the timeline."

"This woman gave me another lady to call, and she said the same thing about Vape. This lady said he was creepy, and she didn't trust him. And that when she heard about the murders, she thought of him right away."

"But she didn't call."

"I know."

"The system have anything on him?"

"I was just about to check."

Derrick was already typing as I said, "All right. I'm going to run someone else through."

"Holy shit, Frank. Guess what Vape was arrested for?"

"Spit it out."

"He was pulled in on a rape charge. Woman claimed she was at a bar, and next thing she knew, she was naked in Vape's house."

I popped out of my chair. "A date rape?"

"That's what it looks like. The accusations were dropped though. The woman didn't want to press charges."

"When was this?"

"Five years ago."

"Anything else on him?"

"No, just the date-rape allegation."

"Give me the woman's contact info."

He handed me the details and said, "Hey, the lab called, guess, uh, they said the picture stolen out of the Chicago gallery matches the one taken from the Crenshaw's Longboat Drive house. It's an exact match: no doubt about it."

"Okay. We'll wrap that up as soon as we get some daylight."

29

—————

TURNING ONTO GRAND LELY DRIVE, I WAS STILL TRYING TO process the fact that someone who'd been arrested for rape was teaching at Florida Southwestern State College. The charges had been dropped, and though I knew there were no legal grounds to dismiss him, I'd hoped that a person responsible for students would somehow be barred.

Intellectually, I knew the thought was pure fantasy, but as a father it was tough to put the brain ahead of the heart. I circled the Collier campus and parked in a lot across from the Health Sciences Hall. A handful of students were relaxing in the shade of an old oak. The scene made me regret that I'd gone to Manhattan's John Jay College of Criminal Justice and not to a place like this.

As agreed, Vape was waiting for me outside the building. He didn't want me to be asking for him. It made me suspicious, but no one wanted it known the police needed to see them.

On the wrong side of fifty, Vape slicked his sandy hair back. His sports jacket was tight across his chest. He extended his hand but didn't look me in the eye.

"Brian Vape."

As we shook, he said to come with him. I followed him into the building and down a brightly lit corridor lined with doors. One of the doors we passed was marked Pharmaceutical Studies. Vape stopped in front of one, unlocked it, and headed behind a metal desk.

Squeezing my way into the chair in front of his desk, I noticed a picture of Abraham Lincoln and a quote attributed to him. Reading it, I knew there was more to worry about regarding what was possibly being taught to our children.

The quote read: "The philosophy of the school room in one generation will be the philosophy of the government in the next."

Vape had mouthed off in Palm Shores in support of euthanasia. Was he using his authority as a professor to indoctrinate students?

"Close the door, please."

Reaching around, I swung the door shut. "Thank you for seeing me."

He picked up one of those reusable water bottles and took a sip before speaking. "I don't have much time; class starts in twenty minutes."

"Are you a doctor?"

"Yes, a radiologist, but I prefer teaching."

I wondered if radiologists could write prescriptions. "I understand you visit your mother often at Palm Shores."

"Yes. That's right."

"And you're aware that two male residents were murdered?"

"Of course. Though I'm not sure they were killed."

"The Collier County Sheriff's Office has determined that foul play was involved."

He didn't react in any way.

"Do you know anyone that might be responsible for the deaths of William Coby and Charles Martin?"

"I barely knew them."

"Based upon your interactions at Palm Shores, does anyone raise suspicion?"

"That nasty Russian aide, for one, and that two-faced janitor."

"Ben Porter?"

He nodded.

"Why do you think either of them would be involved?"

"They're phonies. You know, there's a lot of people around there that make like they're goddamn angels when people are around. But when nobody is looking, they treat the residents like they're garbage. That's why I go every day."

Anyone with their eyes open knew that when family and friends were around, that staff in places like Palm Shores and hospitals were attentive. Not so much when no one was around. It used to drive me crazy visiting someone and hearing the calls for help go unanswered. I guess you had to desensitize yourself to stay sane, much like we officers were forced to do.

"That's good of you. I've been told you're a strong advocate for euthanasia."

"Absolutely. Why it became such a controversial idea is beyond me."

Maybe it was because Jack Kevorkian was spooky-looking. "What makes you believe in it?"

"There's two indisputable facts; it's simply humane to end suffering, and we're spending way too much money supporting lives that lack any quality at all."

"Since we can't afford to keep everyone alive, we should kill them?"

"You're making the same generalized mistake everyone

does. You make it appear that we want to kill off a segment of the population to ensure a higher standard of living for the others. We're living longer these days, which in many cases means we're also having longer deaths. Medical advances are simply keeping people alive longer than their useful life span."

"And euthanizing them is the solution?"

"Do you believe people have a right to a painless death?"

"Yes, but they have medicines to stop pain."

"We believe it stops it, but what about the fact the required dosages put most people into a nonresponsive state?"

I'd seen what he meant and nodded. He had a point.

"Horace said that saving a man's life against his will is to kill him."

"Horace?"

"He was a Roman poet back in the days of Caesar Augustus. He has many famous quotes, like carpe diem."

"The Romans were talking about euthanasia?"

He nodded. "It's a basic human right. If you're a free people, you should have the right to decide when and how you die."

I wasn't sure free was the word to describe people back then.

"Tell me about the trouble you got yourself in."

He stiffened. "There's nothing to say. I'm sure you have the records. The charges were baseless and were dropped."

Time to bluff. "I spoke to Ms. Fields. I'd like to hear your side."

"I don't have the time nor the inclination to talk about a matter that was closed by the courts. I was completely exonerated."

"The charges were dropped; that's very different from being exonerated."

He didn't respond.

"I understand you'd rather not discuss the rape allegation, and I'm not investigating or reopening that case. But there's a connection to the Palm Shore murders."

"Connection? Look, it was an unfortunate situation that I found myself dragged into, and it's over. It was years ago and has nothing to do with what happened to those men."

"Maybe, but I find it curious that the charge against you involved the drug Rohypnol."

"You're fishing, Detective, and wasting time. I've got a class to teach and can't spend any more time enabling your fantastical endeavors."

Vape was not only self-righteous, he was someone whose beliefs justified taking lives. I had to speak with the woman he was accused of raping.

Longboat Drive was less than ten minutes away. Since the Vape interview went shorter than anticipated, I'd pay a visit to the Crenshaws.

Through the front door I saw Robert Crenshaw. He was in a recliner reading a book. When the bell rang, he struggled out of the chair, grabbing his back as he made his way to answer it.

He reached for the handle, hesitating for a moment when he recognized me.

"Good afternoon, Detective. Do you have news for us?"

"No. Just wanted have a quick chat."

"Oh, come in."

"Your back bothering you?"

"Yeah, twisted it reaching for a pen, if you could believe it."

"Been there. Thought you were leaving town?"

"Uh, yeah, we planned to, then, you know, with my back, I didn't want to make it worse flying back to Denver."

He was quicker than I expected with the excuse. But how else would he have afforded a place like this? "The warm weather has to help."

He shrugged. "What did you want to talk about?"

We were standing in the foyer. He was on defense. "You had four paintings that were stolen, right?"

Crenshaw shifted his weight. Was it the back or nerves? "Uh, yeah."

I pulled my phone out. "This is one of them, isn't it?"

He looked at the photo. "You found it? I can't believe it. Sally's going to be so happy. We—"

"No, we didn't find it. Yet. But what I did discover is that your painting was stolen from an art gallery in Chicago."

"What? It can't be."

"Trust me, the lab confirmed it."

"We had nothing to do with the theft."

He didn't challenge the lab assertion. "I'm not saying you did."

"Thank God. We had no idea."

"Really? You paid Visual Universe twenty-five hundred for a painting valued ten times that amount."

"That's all he wanted for it."

"That's because it was hot."

"We had no idea."

"You consider yourself a smart man, don't you?"

"Yes, I'm not a genius, but I—"

"So, you see my point. You had to know it was stolen."

"We didn't. I swear."

"Are you aware that being in possession of stolen goods is a crime?"

"But we didn't know it was stolen."

"I'm going to offer you and your wife an opportunity to cooperate before filing charges against both of you. If you agree to testify that Pierre Robard told you the painting was stolen, you and your wife will go on like nothing happened."

Robard would be the one facing a prison sentence for dealing in stolen goods. If we could locate the stolen painting on his property, the chances were high a judge would slap him with fifteen years behind bars.

30

MY MIND WAS CONSUMED WITH RAGE. NO MATTER HOW I tried, I couldn't get to the place Dr. Bruno wanted me to act from. Hearing what this woman said about her encounter with Brian Vape made me fear for all women, especially my daughter.

Ms. Fields had been at The Parrot Bar and Grill with a girlfriend when Vape began chatting her up. He bought her a drink, and she thought he seemed nice. Her friend saw they were having a good time and took an Uber to another nightspot. Within an hour of her friend's departure, and though she had just two drinks, Fields started feeling drunk.

She didn't recall leaving the bar nor going to Vape's home, where she woke up on his couch, naked. I didn't press, and Fields didn't offer details, but I knew what had happened. Vape had drugged and raped her.

What didn't make sense was the absence of any other complaints against him. Rare is the rapist who does it once. That didn't mean there weren't other victims. Many women, including this one, decided testifying wasn't worth the embarrassment and kept the violation to themselves. I understood the reluctance to relive the devastation, but as a cop, it was frustrating to lose a critical witness.

"Derrick, do me a favor and run a check for civil complaints against Vape."

"I'm on it."

"There was nothing criminal, but maybe a woman filed a lawsuit against him. I'm going up to see how Mary Ann is doing."

"Say hello for me."

Mary Ann was doing good. It was me who needed a break. Vape wasn't home or at work, and until I spoke to him, I had to remain distracted. A quick visit would help. Mary Ann was giving me a hard time on the retirement question.

I knew it was a tough call, and we needed the money. Everyone we spoke with said she'd qualify for disability. That would replace a chunk of her earnings and we'd be fine. The issue was walking away from a career she not only loved but was good at.

Mary Ann had transitioned to a desk job after Jessie was born, and with the danger of being in the streets removed, had planned on another ten years in uniform. I thought she'd be happy to stay home with Jessie, and she wanted to.

The problem was it wasn't on her terms. She didn't say it exactly, but I knew I'd react the same way. I needed to make the important decisions in my life. Having something forced on me was distasteful.

The Sex Crimes Unit was deserted. After being told they were in a meeting, I trudged back downstairs. In the hallway to our office, a janitor was cleaning up water that had flowed in from a backed-up toilet. He didn't look anything like Porter, but my mind settled on the Palm Shores maintenance man.

As Derrick said, there weren't any civil suits with Vape as

a defendant, so I began a search into Ben Porter's son. I hit pay dirt with a couple of keystrokes.

"Guess who owns a string of titty bars in Tampa?" Derrick was rubbing off on me.

"Who's that?"

"Porter's son. Plus he was arrested for distributing marijuana. This kid is a real upstanding citizen."

"So, his old man is living high on dirty money."

"Looks that way. Holy shit! There was a string of dealing arrests made in two of his places. Guess what drugs?"

"Don't tell me roofies."

"Bingo. What are the odds that the maintenance guy at Palm Shores has a son who deals in date-rape drugs?"

"This is convoluted. Even if Porter got the roofies from his son, why overdose someone where he works? It makes no sense."

"We need to find a motive. We get that, and we're on our way. Right now, I don't know what Porter could be up to. Unless he was working with someone like Morley."

"We now have two loose connections to the drug used, and with Vape, we know he's pro euthanasia."

"I don't like the way Porter's been with me. He's lied several times. He's hiding something."

"Maybe it was about his kid."

"I don't know, but I'll find out."

I WAS ADMIRING the orange sky as Mary Ann came onto the lanai with cutlery. She asked, "Is the swordfish ready?"

"Two minutes, max."

"I'll get Jessica."

"I can't believe the homework they gave her. It seems early to be teaching these kids division."

"It's never too early for math. Everything these days, like programming, is math related."

"I guess so. It's been a long time since I did longhand division."

"Do I need to double-check it?"

"Ha-ha. Give me a plate for the fish and get Jessie."

As Mary Ann spooned vegetables onto Jessie's plate, I said, "Look at my Jessie. Tell me one other kid who eats broccoli rabe."

"I like it, Daddy."

Mary Ann set a plate in front of Jessie. "It goes great with swordfish."

Jessie picked up a fork. I said, "Remember, wait till Mom sits and is ready to eat."

Mary Ann said, "Before we eat, I have some news to share."

"Yay! Mommy has a surprise."

I was starving and could eat and listen, but I put my fork down. Mary Ann said, "Mommy is going to take some time off from work. Like a long vacation, and she'll be able to spend a lot of time with you."

"You took a leave?"

She nodded as Jessie screamed her approval.

I was torn. Pissed she hadn't told me in advance, but happy she was putting her health ahead of her heart. "When?"

"End of the month."

"You went to Chester or HR?"

"Chester. He was very supportive, said I could come back whenever I wanted."

I wanted to tell her he'd backpedal if he needed to, but there was no way she'd go back. If and when she got itchy staying home and was up to it, she'd find a job working from home.

Later that night we were laying in bed, unable to sleep. Though we had said good night a half hour ago, I said, "You all right?"

Her voice cracked, "Yeah, guess so."

I rolled on my side and put my arm over her belly. "Everything is going to work out, don't worry."

"I know. I should be happy to spend time with Jessica, but . . ."

I heard myself say, "Taking a leave of absence, which, by the way, is not permanent, is the first change we have to make. Let's hope it's the last, but I get it: it makes things real."

Mary Ann rolled into me and buried her face in my chest, leaving a trail of wetness. "Don't cry, honey. I have a good feeling everything is going to be all right."

She sniffled. "Nobody knows. That's what makes it so scary."

"You know how good my gut is, right?"

I felt her head nod.

I squeezed her. "Then don't worry. All the signals are that this is nothing but a good scare."

Was such a proclamation going to haunt me?

31

———

Thrashing in bed, I said, "No! No!"

"Frank, wake up."

Mary Ann was hovering over me as I came to. "Uh, sorry."

"You're soaking wet. You dreaming about Barrow?"

I shrugged. I wished it were about my first homicide case, where I allowed myself to get bullied into the arrest of an innocent kid. We didn't have enough on him, but afraid to buck the lead detective, I went along. It felt shitty when I agreed to arrest him, unbearable when the kid hung himself the first night he was behind bars, and crippling when it turned out he didn't do it.

"Sorry I woke you." Barrow had haunted me for years, but the nightmare I just had was even more personal.

"It's okay. I got to go to the bathroom."

I lay back down, and the vision of Mary Ann in a hospital bed rushed back. She was unable to move or communicate and was losing the ability to eat and drink effectively. I was standing over her with a glass—a drink laced with drugs that would end her suffering—and her life.

Positioning the straw between her lips, I swiped away a tear rolling down her cheek. Our eyes locked as she struggled to suck up the brew. My tears pelted her face as Jessie began sobbing.

Mary Ann's head lolled, and I yanked the straw from her mouth. I shook her, but she was gone. I had killed her.

Rubbing my eyes, I got up, passing Mary Ann on the way to the bathroom. Sitting on the toilet, I wondered how anyone could kill someone they loved and not be haunted by nightmares. Maybe it was my Catholic upbringing stressing the sanctity of life that made it impossible to help someone die, even if they were in pain.

Perched on the bowl, I remembered a guy named Marino who was on the force with me in New Jersey. His wife had been in a horrific car accident and was in a coma.

It was as bad a situation as you could imagine. Marino took a leave for the first month before returning to work. A week later, it was determined that all activity in her brain had ceased. She was brain dead.

Though there was no hope of a recovery, he couldn't make the decision to take her off life support. Seeing him each day was tough. He was aging right before our eyes. Normally, West Point erect, Marino developed the stoop of an eighty-year-old.

As the flow of urine ebbed, I recalled it took him six months to pull the plug. Tough as it was, he made the right call. The entire department attended the funeral. I didn't know if it was the show of support or the removal of the burden, but Marino regained most of his posture before his wife was in the ground.

After washing, I climbed back into bed. Mary Ann was already out. Closing my eyes, I knew it would be a struggle to get back to sleep. I fought to keep an image of the Gulf of Mexico in my head. It took practice, but it usually relaxed me.

———

THE COFFEE DERRICK brought me each morning wasn't a cure for cancer, but it was exactly what I needed, especially today. I put the cup to my lips as Derrick said, "The team got to Robard's house about ten minutes ago. Robard wasn't there."

I nodded.

"Late night?"

"Couldn't sleep."

"What's the matter? It's not Mary Ann, is it?"

"She's okay. Just thinking too much, that's all."

"I had a nightmare myself last night."

How did he know? "What about?"

"Lynn and I were on a Ferris wheel all the way at the top and it got stuck. Lynn was being rescued and started to fall. I tried to catch her, but I was too late."

"Ugh."

"Was yours about Mary Ann?"

I nodded and told him about my dream.

"You have a lot of stuff running through your head, Frank. It's normal."

"What do you really think about euthanasia?"

"I'm against it but only because of the slippery slope thing. Where would it stop? Who would decide what's a worthy life?"

"What if someone is brain dead, in a coma, or so incapacitated they can't move?"

"If you're brain dead, then okay. But otherwise, I say no.

Look at that scientist, Stephen Hawking. I don't think he could move anything except his eyes, but he still made amazing discoveries."

I took a gulp of coffee. "That's a good point, but we're not going to solve the issue today. Do me a favor and check if radiologists can write prescriptions."

"I know they can."

"How do you know that?"

"My cousin's a radiologist. He went to med school, just like every doctor."

"You sure about the scripts?"

"Yep, he used to write them whenever my aunt got sick."

I Googled it anyway. He was right, Vape could write prescriptions. It wasn't a big deal, as Rohypnol was easy to get on the streets. He wasn't the type to mingle with drug dealers, but there'd be a record if he chose to write a script.

Was it worth my time looking for proof he'd authorized the drug he may have used to rape Fields? If I had run the rape investigation, it would have been the first thing I did.

It wouldn't have been as easy at that time, though, as programs to monitor the issuance of prescriptions hadn't existed. Watchdog entities had been created recently in an attempt to tamp down the opioid crisis. It was a terrible example of good coming out of bad, but it was a helpful tool to identify rogue physicians.

The possible crime by Vape was not something I was going to try to hold him accountable for. The value it held was the alarm it sounded. If Vape was the killer, investing time in the old case wasn't going to solve the homicides. That would require a fresh approach. The problem was I didn't have another angle to pursue.

The phone rang. Derrick had a quick chat and hung up. "They found the painting. It was under a bed."

"That's enough for a second-degree felony charge. Get an arrest warrant out for Robard. I'll let the sheriff know and get him to have special crimes take it from here. We have to catch this killer before he strikes again."

32

___

The food was on the table. I picked up the remote to shut the lanai TV when a "breaking news" banner floated behind a newscaster: "This just in. There's been a report of an attempted murder at Palm Shores."

"What the fuck?"

"Frank! What's wrong with you?"

"Daddy said a bad word."

"Uh, I'm sorry. It just slipped out. Look at this garbage." I pointed to the TV. A reporter was standing in front of Palm Shores: "Less than twenty minutes ago, we received an anonymous call that an attempt to kill a woman living here had occurred. We're working to obtain further details, but what we know is that an assailant attempted to suffocate a female resident in her room. The management of Palm Shores has not responded to a request for an interview."

As he droned on about the Cobb and Martin murders, my cell vibrated. It was Chester. "You guys eat. I have to take this; it's the sheriff."

"Luca, get down to Palm Shores. It appears an assault has occurred."

"Just saw it on the news. They said it was an attempted suffocation. I don't think it's related to our case, but I'll head down and check it out."

"Keep it as quiet as you can."

It's on TV and he wants it kept quiet? "Yes, sir."

"If, in fact, this assault occurred, the perpetrator must be apprehended immediately. You still haven't solved the other murders."

Still? The investigation was just over a month old. "We're working on several angles."

"Your last report was light on details. What do you have?"

"We have two people of interest with strong links to the drug used in the murders."

"That's promising. What's the timeline?"

"It's difficult to say, but we're making good progress."

"Put this to bed, Luca, or you'll be the one addressing the media."

He knew how much I hated holding press conferences. "Yes, sir."

"Keep me apprised."

He hung up before I could say good night. I slid open the door and stepped onto the lanai.

"Everything all right?"

"Yeah, the sheriff wants me to look into that report."

"You're leaving, Daddy?"

"After dinner. I'll be back before your bedtime, so take care of Mommy until I get back, okay?"

She returned my wink. The kid was too cute for words.

ONE OF TWO marked cars pulled out of the driveway as I arrived. A dozen residents were huddled into two groups. It was seven forty-five. On a normal night, half of them would be sleeping in front of a TV.

All eyes were on me as Murphy, the responding officer, summarized the situation. The alleged attack was made on Cecilia Robbins, an eighty-four-year-old resident who lived on the second floor of the main building. When he told me who the suspect was, I shook my head in disbelief.

I told Murphy to make sure no one left the premises and went to see Mrs. Robbins. Morley was standing by the bar in the main living room. The area was crowded with residents who, undoubtedly, were discussing the new charge. No one seemed afraid, which I found odd, as I approached the apartment where the attack occurred.

A bald man in his fifties with a beer belly answered the door. "Can I help you?"

I stuck my badge out. "Detective Luca, Collier County Sheriff's Office. I'd like to speak to Cecilia Robbins."

He peered over his glasses at my credentials before saying, "Come in. I'm her son, Timothy. Mother is resting in her bedroom."

I followed him and the growing sound of a loud TV. If she was resting, she had to be deaf.

Covers up to her neck and mouth agape, Robbins was fast asleep. Her son grabbed the remote off a pile of mail on the nightstand and shut the TV.

He jostled the small-framed lady awake. "Mother, this is a detective from the sheriff's office. He needs to ask you a couple of questions. Do you feel up to it?"

Robbins swept her glasses off the nightstand and propped herself up as her son made the introductions. Gray was showing where she parted her short hair.

"I'd like you to tell me exactly what happened earlier this evening."

"Like I told the police officer, I was getting ready for bed. I've been very tired the last week or so. The doctor's been adjusting my thyroid medication, and it's had an awful effect on me."

"Mother had a precancerous nodule removed right before she moved in here."

"How long have you been here, Ms. Robbins?"

"A week after the news about those poor men. I tell you, I would never have moved in. I tried to get my money back, but they wouldn't hear it. They were going to keep forty thousand dollars of my money if I didn't move in. My husband and I worked hard for what we have, and I wasn't going to give it away. Now, after tonight, I should have."

Her blue eyes were clear and she seemed lucid. "You gave Palm Shores a large deposit, opting for a lower monthly fee?"

She nodded, but her son said, "Sixty thousand. I told Mother not to do it, but she wouldn't listen."

Robbins stared at her son. She may have been in her eighties, but she could still burn a hole with her eyes.

I said, "Please tell me what happened tonight."

"I had dinner downstairs and came up to watch *Wheel of Fortune*. When it was over, I went to get the mail. And then Timothy called as I was coming back with the mail." She glanced at the nightstand. "I didn't even get a chance to go through it."

"So, after dinner, you came up, left the apartment to get the mail, then spoke on the phone with your son. Then what?"

"Well, I was tired. I even told Timothy that, and after hanging up, I washed up and got in bed."

"What happened next?"

"I think I might have dozed off for a second, and when I woke up, he was there with a pillow to suffocate me. He tried to kill me."

"Who was it?"

"Porter."

"Are you referring to Ben Porter, the maintenance man?"

"Yes. How can they let someone like him work here?"

"When you saw him, what did you do?"

"I screamed. Told him to get the hell out of my house. And I rang my alarm." She fingered a red plastic pendant hanging around her neck.

"What did Mr. Porter do?"

"He took off like the coward he is. Shame on him for attacking a defenseless woman."

"Did he put the pillow over your face?"

"No, I woke up too soon."

"You said he held a pillow by your bedside. What made you think he was going to use it to suffocate you?"

"Come on, Detective, what do you think he was going to do with it? He was holding it like this." She grabbed the pillow from behind her and held it between her hands. "Just like in the movies."

"And you're certain he intended to harm you?"

"Absolutely. You should have seen his eyes. They were pure evil."

It was a serious charge that needed vetting. Leaving Robbins' apartment, I was accosted by a resident. What she told me made the blood in my ears pound.

33

———

Porter was sitting in the small café off the main room. He was chatting in French with an overweight security guard as if he didn't have a care in the world. I heard the word football as I entered. They were probably talking about a soccer game. I asked the guard to leave.

Shutting the French doors to the room, I said, "You were speaking French."

"Nah, man. That's Creole, but I know French. They're similar."

Porter spoke three languages. It was safe to assume he lied in all of them. I sat next to him. "You want to explain what you were doing in Ms. Robbins' apartment?"

"I was on my way to the Conways to replace a bulb. They're a couple of doors down from Ms. Robbins."

His presence on the floor was verifiable. I nodded.

"I saw her door open."

"Her front door was open?"

"Yeah, I stuck my head in and called, but she didn't answer. I don't know if she couldn't hear me because the TV was on or if something had happened to her."

"So, you entered?"

He shook his head. "I probably shouldn't have, but if I didn't and something was wrong . . ."

"After you went in, what did you do?"

"I was asking if she was okay. Nobody was answering. I went into her bedroom, and it looked like she was sleeping. I got close to make sure she was breathing. A bunch of mail was on the floor, and one of her pillows was on the floor too. I picked them up. She woke up and started screaming. I tried to calm her down, but she wouldn't, so I left."

"She claims you were about to put the pillow over her face."

"That's crazy, man. She's an old lady, making things up. These people create more trouble than they're worth."

"They're better off dead?"

"That's not what I meant. I was saying I shouldn't have bothered worrying if she was okay or not. See where it got me?"

"You claim her door was open when you just happened to be walking by."

"That's right."

"Do you have a key to her apartment?"

His shoulders sagged. "Come on, man. I have master keys for every apartment here."

"Was there anyone else in the hallway at the time?"

"I didn't see anybody. But people here, they're always poking their heads out the door, seeing what's going on."

"So, no one to back up your story that the door was left open?"

"I'm telling you how it was, man."

"Why don't you tell me how it is with your son?"

He blinked. "What do you mean? He has nothing to do with this."

"You didn't mention he owns a couple of strip clubs in Tampa."

"What he does for a living is his business. I don't like it, but he's an adult; he does what he wants."

Maybe it was because I was in law enforcement, or maybe it was because I was a newish father and ignorant, but there was no way my kid was going to get involved in a morally bankrupt business.

"What do you know about his drug dealing?"

"He runs bars. Francois doesn't deal drugs. He never even tried them. He got pulled in 'cause they were dealing in his place."

"I find it interesting that the drug he was busted for was one and the same that was used to kill Coby and Martin."

He averted his eyes. "I don't know nothing about that."

There was something there, but what? "Tell me again what happened."

He kept to his story about seeing Robbins' door open and wondering if something had happened to her. He claimed to have called her name, but the TV might have covered his voice. I'd heard the volume of the TV she watched or slept to. As for the pillow, he swore that he was only picking up what had fallen.

I constructed a plausible scenario: Robbins had gone out for the mail. If her son was calling as she returned to the apartment, she may have gotten distracted and forgotten to close the door. Porter entering to check on an elderly resident could've been simply a nice gesture. He didn't deny holding the pillow, saying he was just picking up what had fallen. Part of his duties were janitorial; it could have been instinctual.

Countering a possible misunderstanding was the fact that Porter had a key to her place. Robbins was also a newcomer who wanted to back out of moving in. She was scared because of the murders. Would an older woman, afraid for her safety, forget to close the door to her apartment? Then there was the money.

Palm Shores stood to pocket her deposit of sixty thousand. Could there be an alliance between Porter and Morley? Had Porter changed his MO from overdosing to smothering since we uncovered the poisonings?

Morley was behind the bar looking more like the director of entertainment than an executive. I caught his eye and he waved. I beckoned with my hand. He pointed at his chest as if to say, who, me? and I nodded. He took his time, interacting with a couple of residents as he made his way. The thought he should run for office ran through my head.

"I understand Ms. Robbins was confused about this evening's events. It's something we're used to in this business. Father Time can be cruel."

He may be cruel, but most of us were more worried that he was undefeated. "The responding officer was told there are no surveillance cameras in the hallway."

"That's true. Believe me, I'd love to have them, but the residents feel it's an invasion of their privacy."

"Tell me about Ben Porter."

"There's not much to say. He's been with us for years and is an exemplary employee. It's fair to say everyone here not only gets along with him but enjoys his presence. I wish I could find more like him."

"Have there been any other incidents involving Mr. Porter and a resident?"

"I'm not sure I understand your question, Detective."

"A situation where a resident felt threatened by Mr. Porter?"

"Quite the contrary. I believe he's a comforting presence at Palm Shores."

Walking toward the front doors, I was about to classify this as a misunderstanding when I heard a pattering of squeaky footsteps. I turned around. It was Galena Vuvich. What she told me not only changed my mind but amped up the conspiracy possibility.

34

Doing an about-face, I marched back into the great room. Morley's shoulders sagged when he saw me.

"Something else, Detective?"

I kept my voice low. "Your damn right there is. I asked you specifically if there were other threatening incidents involving Porter and a resident."

"There weren't any."

"I was just informed that a former resident believed Porter tried to kill her by flooding her apartment with gas."

"First of all, that was over two years ago. We looked into it but couldn't substantiate the claim."

"Who is we?"

"Palm Shores, myself included."

"Anyone with a law enforcement background?"

He shook his head. "No, but we didn't believe it was necessary. You see—"

"Did she file a complaint with the sheriff's office?"

"No, I don't believe so. You see, Mrs. Holloway was prone to believing someone was either stealing from her or wanted to hurt her."

"Give me your side of it."

"As I mentioned, it was over two years ago, so forgive me if I'm foggy on some of it."

"Let's hear it."

"It was well after dinner, and one of her children, I believe it was her eldest son, came to drop off clothing or something. When he entered her room, he smelled gas. His mother had fallen asleep watching TV. He took her into the hallway and went back in to open the sliders. When he went into the kitchen, he noticed the stove switched on but no flame. He shut it down and that was that."

"Why was Porter suspected?"

"Earlier that evening, Mrs. Holloway had reported she was having trouble with the stove's knobs. I believe she claimed one had fallen off. We created a repair ticket, and Porter was sent to check on it."

"And what was wrong?"

"A knob was loose. He made a simple adjustment."

"And that was it?"

"Yes, he left right after fixing it."

"He'd have to put the burner on to test the knob."

"I imagine so. But what we think happened was that after Porter left, Mrs. Holloway went to see if it worked, and for whatever reason, left the gas running without the burner on."

"How could something like that happen? Isn't there a safety switch or something to prevent that?"

"I honestly don't know. We had the appliance repairman come, but he found there was nothing wrong with it. It could just be one of those things that happen from time to time. But if Mrs. Holloway was, shall we say, completely with it, she would never have left it on."

"She reported Porter as the one who left it on?"

"Yes. But I don't think the son even believed her claim that Porter was trying to kill her."

"I understand she felt so threatened by the incident that she moved out."

"That's not accurate. You see, her dementia was progressing rapidly, and we're not really set up to handle those challenges. Our mission is to provide the highest level of active living for seniors. A platinum experience for their golden years."

As long as they had a sack of gold bullion to pay for it. "What type of contract did Mrs. Holloway sign with Palm Shores?"

"I'm not sure I understand the question."

"Did she make a down payment, opting for lower monthly fees?"

"I'm sorry, but I don't recall her particular plan."

I was betting the woman had handed over a substantial share of her savings. "I'd appreciate the details on her arrangements with you."

His face dropped into a frown before he recovered. "I'll have the records pulled."

"Now, I'd like to have another word with Porter. Can you locate him for me?"

A resident walked by holding a coffee cup. It smelled amazing.

"I'll have him paged." He signaled a woman standing a few feet away. "Where would you like to speak to him?"

"Tell him I'll meet him back in the café."

I started toward the café but wanted to text Mary Ann. As I started typing, I overheard Morley and the woman.

Morley said, "Page Ben Porter. Tell him to go to the café."

"Will do. And Ryan finally called in."

"Where the hell was he?"

"He didn't say."

"Is he going to be in tomorrow?"

"He said he would."

"Okay, go page Porter."

It was more proof that Morley had his hands full. It made sense that he wanted to sell. But had he concocted a scheme to juice the payoff? Was Porter playing a major role in it?

I sent a text to Mary Ann telling her I'd be home within the hour. Her response was a curt okay. I apologized and said I'd get home as soon as possible.

Guilt flooded my head. I was failing the "being there for her" covenant. Walking back to the café, I began blaming Chester for calling my house when he knew our situation.

The gap in Porter's front teeth seemed wider as he smiled. "You forget something, man?"

"Sit down."

As he sat, I detected the smell of marijuana. Either he was innocent and unworried enough to smoke a joint, or he was looking to calm his nerves after our first chat. "Not even twenty minutes ago, I asked you about any other incidents, and you said there were no others."

"Uh-huh. That's right."

"What about Mrs. Holloway and the gas in her apartment?"

"That was long ago, man. The old lady, she was losing her mind, you know?"

The yellow in the whites of his eyes was tinged red. "Tell me what happened."

"It was nothing. She was having a problem with one knob. I think she played around with it too much, you know? It was loose, almost stripped, so I put some glue on it. Took a minute, that's all."

"Did you turn the burner on?"

"Yeah, I showed her it was working, no problem."

"When you left, did you shut the burner?"

"Yeah, I only put it on for a second to show her."

"Why would she think you left it on?"

"She's old; can't help herself."

"Mrs. Holloway believed you were trying to kill her."

He smiled. "She's going around the bend, man. Like half the people here. The old people, are like, nice one minute and then crazy, you know?"

"Why is that you always seem to be the one being accused?"

"I'm from Jamaica, man. They don't understand us, you know?"

He was right as far as he was concerned. I hadn't been able to unravel what kind of man he was and what he was capable of. Right now, there were just too many coincidences for me to feel comfortable.

Porter had lied. He had a son with a record and a business where Rohypnol was dealt. He was involved in at least two incidents putting residents at risk. He was my number-one person of interest.

I needed to get home and as I climbed in the Cherokee the warning Vuvich gave me about Morley and Porter rang in my ears.

35

———————

As I sped home, I rolled around the pair of incidents involving Porter. Were there others involving him or someone else that had slipped by? A death caused by something like gas poisoning would have to be reported, but what about the pillow episode?

Had suffocation deaths been classified as natural or had they been attributed to heart attacks? How would we know now? Way more attention needed to be focused on deaths in all facilities. I now realized that, too often, death certificates were signed without an eye for foul play because of the age of the deceased.

That there were thousands of deranged people roaming around was discounted because the deaths occurred inside facilities that were supposed to be safe. This despite the reality that killers hid in plain sight. They've always been our neighbors, coworkers, and friends.

It worried me, but what was more unsettling was a relatively new concern. Enormous amounts of money could be made from older people dying earlier than they naturally should. It was a revelation to me. I was certain everyone thought money was being minted by the health care and assisted living industries.

What very few people understood was that a new model for housing the aging wealthy had been developed. This scheme had seniors turning over hundreds of thousands of dollars to the operators of luxury and upmarket housing. Some of the newer places, like Moorings Park, were difficult to get into, and the payment was akin to an initiation fee. In other establishments, residents traded a bundle of cash for lower monthly rates. Who knew what other ways would crop up to get seniors to part with their money?

In either case, the exchange was ripe for fraud and even murder. I had to take a closer look at greed as a motivating factor.

IT WAS after Jessie's bedtime when I got back home. I expected to find Mary Ann on the couch watching TV, but she wasn't in the family room. I headed into the bedroom, but she wasn't there either. The lights on the lanai were out, and that left Jessie's bedroom.

Mary Ann was in the rocking chair staring at our sleeping daughter. I tiptoed in and whispered, "You okay?"

She looked up. Her eyes were wet.

I grabbed her hand. "Come on. Let's not wake her up."

We sat on the couch, and though I knew what was bothering her, said, "What's the matter?"

She shrugged. "I'm scared, not for me but for Jessica. I mean, I want to be there for her as she grows up."

"You will be."

"I don't know, Frank. If this gets worse, it's going to change everything. I want to be able to do things with her."

"You will. What won't you be able to do?"

"I don't know, in ten years she'll be going to the prom, and half the excitement is shopping for a dress, and I'll probably be in a wheelchair or worse by then. And I'll—"

"Hold on. That's nonsense and you know it. You're going to be fine. There's all kind of treatments these days."

She slumped into me. A tear dropped onto my hand.

"Don't cry, honey."

"Why is this happening to us?"

"I know it's scary, but we're in this together, and we're going to be fine. Especially Jessie. She going to be better than fine."

"Promise me you'll take care of her."

"Of course I will. But stop being ridiculous. Both of us are going to bring her up."

"I don't want to be the one to hold her back. I don't want her worrying about me—"

"Hold on a second."

"I'm sorry."

"It's okay." I kissed her cheek. "The bottom line is we have an unpredictable situation on our hands. It may get challenging, but together we'll get through whatever comes our way—if it comes our way."

She looked me in the eye. "You think I'm going be one of the unlucky ones?"

"You have me and Jessie. How can you be unlucky?"

"Seriously, Frank, what do you think?"

"We're facing an unknown with MS. But what we do know is how to adjust. We'll do what we have to, and everything will work out."

"But if it gets bad, what's going to happen to us, to me and you?"

"Nothing, this will only make us stronger. There's nobody I would rather be with than you."

"You're just saying that."

"No, I'm not. Did you forget I was married before?"

She shrugged.

"You can count on me, Mary Ann. We have a lot to worry about, but don't ever worry about me. I'm always going to be there for you and Jessie."

THE NEXT MORNING, pulling into Palm Shores, I noticed the Bentley belonging to the salesman Hall was sloppily parked. If an old-timer pulled in next to him, Hall would get a thousand-dollar dent. Ever the protector, I parked alongside him. Squeezing out of the Cherokee, I looked inside the Bentley. A messy array of empty fast-food bags and cups lay in the passenger wheel well. I headed inside.

I followed the music into an all-purpose room. A man in a cowboy hat was strumming a guitar behind a karaoke track. His deep voice sang, "Because you're mine."

And a handful of residents responded, "I walk the line."

He sounded like Johnny Cash. Foot tapping, I spied Vuvich talking to a staffer in the corner of the room. Her cowboy boots clashed with the ornate cross hanging from her neck.

When the entertainer segued into "A Boy Named Sue," Vuvich began singing. The singer waved her over and they sang together. She was having fun but didn't add to the performance. I stepped farther into the room and she noticed. When the song ended, she waddled over.

"Galena love Johnny Cash."

Never a big fan, I'd recently seen a documentary about him and was impressed. "He was good."

"You want to talk to Galena?"

I nodded, and we stepped into the hallway. "You've worked here a while?"

"Seven and one-half years."

"I want to know if you remember any situation involving possible harm, even if it's one in a million."

"Like the gas, I told you?"

"Exactly. Think about it. And not just anything involving Ben Porter. Anyone, Fred Morley, Ryan Hall, even visitors or vendors of Palm Shores."

"Ryan is good boy, but he is maybe drinking too much."

Was he driving drunk again? "Does anyone, like Mr. Morley, know about that?"

"Maybe he does, but Morley protects Ryan, like son."

"I see. Now, were there any unusual circumstances where someone was hurt or could have been?"

"This was long time ago. Galena was part time then, so six years, maybe. Mrs. McCarthy drowned in pool in the middle of night."

"How did that happen?"

She shrugged. "Galena was at other job. They say the Mrs. McCarthy was drunk and fell in."

"No one witnessed it?"

"They said no."

"No camera coverage?"

"Galena don't know, but Mrs. McCarthy drink too much. I see her that day, drinking with Brian Vape."

What? "Mr. Vape was here back then?"

"His mother just move in from other place. They kick her out."

"Vape's mother was thrown out of another facility? Why?"

She fingered her cross. "Brian Vape, he has no soul. Always talking about the euthanasia. You know, the place didn't want him coming anymore."

"What was the name of the facility where she was at before?"

"In Cape Coral, but Galena don't remember name."

MARY ANN WAS CURLED up on the couch. She looked beat. I wanted to tell Jessie to stop playing with the little keyboard we got her, but she said, "Daddy! Watch me. I know how to play 'Mary Had a Little Lamb.'"

Mary Ann eked out a smile. "Great. Hang on a second. Daddy has to talk to Mommy for a minute."

"You okay?"

"Been getting a stabbing pain in my face. Right here." She pointed to a spot just below her cheekbone.

"How long has this been going on?"

"Started a couple of days ago, but it's gotten worse today."

Last night's semimeltdown now made sense. "Did you call the doctor?"

"I looked it up. It's just one of the symptoms of MS."

My stomach dropped. She was getting an attack already? The way the doctors talked, it seemed like it would be in the future sometime, if at all.

"I'm calling the doctor. Let's get in to see him. Maybe there's something they can do to ease the pain."

"I'll call. Pay attention to Jessica."

The promise I made to myself to be present whenever I

was around Jessie was impossible to keep. As she pressed keys that lit up, guiding her through the tune, my mind tumbled into doom. Was this the beginning? Was Mary Ann one of the unlucky ones whose illness would escalate rapidly?

"Did you like it, Daddy?"

"Oh. It was wonderful. I, I can't believe you learned that. I'm so proud of you."

"I'm going to learn happy birthday for Mommy."

How many more birthdays did my wife have left? What kind of shape would she be in? Would she be able to blow out her own candles?

"That's great. Hold on a minute; I have to call work. It's very important. I'll be right back."

I slipped out the front door and made a call.

"Doc, you have a minute?"

"Sure. What's going on?"

"It's Mary Ann. She's been getting a stabbing feeling in her face. What do you think?"

"Hmm. The first thing, don't panic. MS attacks come and go. This might just go away by itself, but make an appointment with her neurologist."

"Mary Ann is. But what do you think it means?"

"It could be MS related or simply a dental issue."

"But you think it's the MS, right?"

"I don't know, Frank. Mary Ann has been diagnosed with MS, and she could be experiencing an episode of trigeminal neuralgia."

"There's a chance it could be a dental problem, right?"

"Why don't you wait until she's examined. I know it's difficult, but try not to get worked up until you know exactly what's going on."

I walked up the block trying to process the development.

Bilotti was right about waiting, but he wasn't the one that had to mark time for two days.

As I passed Ronnie's house, I thought about what his dead father had said at the last barbecue before moving into Palm Shores. He didn't know much about wine but loved his two glasses a day. I kidded with him, asking if that was his secret to a long life.

His dad got serious and said it was all about worrying. He said it took a lot out of you and that no matter how much worrying you did, it would never change a thing. He went on to say it was like practicing disappointment.

I knew Bill Coby was a wise man, but I didn't know he could reach me from the afterworld.

36

Thunder boomed as I spoke on the phone with the Lee County Sheriff's Office. We needed more information on the activities of Porter's son. I'd requested the arrest records a week ago, and they still hadn't been sent.

As I was getting an assurance they'd be sent within the hour, Derrick came into the office. His shirt was soaked.

"You got caught, huh?"

"Yeah, but it was worth it. Guess what I found out?"

Having gotten jerked around by the bureaucrats in Lee County, I was less than thrilled to take a shot at mind reading. All I could muster was a sigh.

"Okay, but you're not going to believe this. I'd hate for it to be true, but Water's Edge, the place where Vape's mother was before going to Palm Shores, had a string of odd deaths."

"Odd? In what way?"

"Every one of them died within days of their ninetieth birthday."

"How many people we talking about?"

"Three. All men."

"What was the listed cause of death?"

"Heart failure."

"Were they otherwise healthy?"

"They seemed to be."

"All right, run them down. Talk with the families; grab their medical records, if you can. Let's see if there are any common threads."

"You got it."

"And Vape's mother was there when they died?"

"Yep. The first death was ten weeks, then eight, and the last, two weeks before she moved out."

I shook my head, trying to process the information, when Derrick asked, "You think he killed them because of their age?"

"Being ninety may be some sort of twisted marker for him."

"But Martin and Coby were in their mid-eighties, not that close to ninety."

"I know, but maybe he ramped up his crusade. Or it could just be a coincidence."

"I don't know. Why wouldn't he do in his own mother, then? He'd get an inheritance in addition to getting his rocks off."

"Because his mother provides access to prey. If his mom is dead, how is he going to get into these places enough times to know the lay of the land? There's a fair amount of planning going on, otherwise it would, or should have been, detected."

"I never heard of a serial killer with this kind of motivation. Have you?"

"There was a woman doctor, in Brazil, I think, who killed up to three hundred patients. She felt they weren't dying fast enough to free up beds for people who needed them."

"Playing God."

"No doubt. But on some crazy level, I kind of get it. The

people she killed were near death, and the hospital had no space to take in people who were sick but not terminal. I get her reasoning, but that would be a helluva slippery slope to get on. What happens when the near dead are killed, and they still need beds? Who's next? Anyone with a disability?"

"It's some sort of return to the Middle Ages. When people got sick, they took them outside the city walls to die. It was so cruel. Can you imagine?"

"They were afraid they'd catch whatever was going on, like the plague. They had no way to know what was contagious or how to cure most illnesses. Did you ever see how crude the medical care was?"

"It was primitive. Bloodletting, hacking limbs off without anesthesia. God, just thinking about it gives me the willies."

"We need to get a lot more information on who Brian Vape is. If he's on some kind of euthanasia mission, there's got to be signs."

"Should we put a tail on him?"

"Not yet. What we have now seems to indicate that he's not out there killing people in the open. And we don't have any elderly unsolves—that we know about."

"I hate to say it, but we haven't been looking. These deaths at Water's Edge would have stayed unnoticed if we didn't start poking around. You want me to start with Vape's neighbors and friends?"

"Yeah, get moving. I hope to God it's just a crazy coincidence, but if it's not, we got to nail him before he kills again."

I couldn't help thinking that if something like this was suspected to have happened in or near a school, the authorities would shut it down in a heartbeat. It was the right policy, but weren't seniors just as vulnerable?

Derrick grabbed his jacket and left me pondering how to wrap this up quickly. Normally, Chester was up my butt about solving a homicide. The sheriff was pressing, but I could deal with him. What I couldn't deal with was a major time suck when my family needed me around.

A new email pinged. It was from Dr. Bilotti. He wanted to let me know about a new treatment study for MS that had commenced at Johns Hopkins University. He said it was an entirely new path being undertaken, one that focused not on treating the disease but on curing it.

He provided a link but cautioned that it was a long shot. He simply wanted to show me there were many efforts being researched. Opening the link, I read the short article on the study. It was light on specifics but heavy on the revolutionary and necessary approach to find a cure.

Looking around the site, I clicked onto a piece about the controversy surrounding a new drug to treat Alzheimer's. Months ago, the drug company had pulled its application on a promising treatment due to a lack of data supporting its effectiveness.

Reassessing the results of the clinical trials, the pharmaceutical company discovered that certain patients, taking the highest doses, had less memory loss than those untreated. There were tons of statistics, but it looked like a fifth of the patients afflicted had positive results.

Emboldened by the findings, they reapplied to the FDA for approval to sell the expensive drug. It seemed like finding a diamond in a sand dune, and it raised my hopes—until I read a comment below the article.

The commenter feared that having Medicare pay for expensive treatments for a thin slice of the population would speed up the bankruptcy of the program. He also said as Medicare went bust, the financial strain would crowd out funding for other vital services that Medicare paid for, meanwhile the drug company would profit while the population at large suffered.

It was a valid concern, but like most people, I wanted the advancements in medicine to continue. That meant the drug companies had to make money to keep hunting for cures. I didn't care what the cost was and who made what, if there was something that would help my wife, I wanted it. Now.

37

———

Derrick had run down the medical records for the deceased at Water's Edge. The three were taking the usual slew of medicines but were in as good a state of health as you could expect at ninety.

Without the bodies or other physical evidence, it was impossible to determine if foul play was involved. Vape was a doctor, and his mother had lived in a senior community for five years. How much would he know about how they handled deaths? Did he believe he'd found the perfect way to kill?

If the administrator, who had no love for Brian Vape and his euthanasia crusade, hadn't mentioned it, we'd never know about the coincidental deaths. The question was this: Was she creating noise as payback; was it coincidental timing, or was it murder?

I was at a crossroads. Discarding the possibility the deaths were natural would focus the Palm Shore murders on Porter. Such a narrow focus didn't feel right, not yet.

We needed more info on Vape. The problem was his neighbors claimed he was a loner, and there was no family. I decided to focus on his work life and picked up the phone to find someone who knew Brian Vape.

RAY BULLARD HAD KNOWN Vape for twenty years. The two of them met in medical school and had roomed together. He was a radiologist at Physicians Regional Medical Care's Pine Ridge campus. I swung off Napa Boulevard into a shopping center and pulled into a space near Giovanni's Ristorante.

It was a cloudless day, and the restaurant seemed darker than usual. My eyes adjusted as the hostess led me to a table where Bullard waited. The smell of pizza was in the air. We shook hands, and I slid into the booth.

"You come here a lot?"

Bullard shrugged. "When I'm at this campus, I do." He patted his stomach. "But the pasta is adding up."

He didn't have much to worry about. Bullard was ten pounds away from wiry. His sandy hair was thinning, and he had a sharp nose. "Tell me about it. Look, I know you're busy. Order your lunch and we'll talk."

He glanced at the menu and snapped it shut. I was hoping he'd order a pizza. The waiter took his Insalata di Mare. I recalled how good they made it here, but I had a Tupperware with chicken salad sitting in the office fridge.

"As I said, I'm looking into Brian Vape. What can you tell me about him?"

"We went to med school together, even shared an apartment for two years. He's a smart guy. I don't know why he stopped practicing. It could have been the pushback management gave him."

"He was disciplined at the hospital?"

"He couldn't separate his personal beliefs from his job.

After the agony of what his father went through, it was difficult for him to keep his mouth shut."

"Can you explain?"

"Sure. His father had bone cancer and suffered for years. It traveled to his spine, and that's about as painful a situation as you could imagine. It affected Brian. He began getting interested in euthanasia and started saying things the hospital didn't appreciate."

"That's when he left to teach?"

"Yep, he went to Florida Southwestern."

"Did you still keep in touch?"

"Yeah, I mean, we drifted a bit since we didn't work together, but we'd still see each other. He was turning into a loner though, especially when the Euthanasia Society folded up."

It wasn't surprising to hear, and it wasn't illegal either. "He belonged to that organization?"

"Yep." The waiter set down Bullard's seafood salad and a basket of bread. When he asked me if I was sure I didn't want anything, it was hard to say no.

"He seems devoted to his mother."

"Yeah, he's a good son. I don't know if he still goes every day, but he used to."

"You don't talk with him anymore?"

Bullard shrugged. "He became a bit weird, especially when he formed an organization after the euthanasia one collapsed. It was something like, the Partnership for Caring. Has a nice ring, doesn't it? But I guess that was the point."

Vape was instrumental in the successor to the Euthanasia Society of America? "He created it?"

"That's what he told me. Not alone though. There's quite a few people these days who believe like he does."

"Did he ever talk about taking a life?"

Holding a piece of bread, Bullard stopped mid-dip. A pregnant pause, big enough for triplets, ensued before he said, "No. He never spoke about anything like that. There's no doubt he's a strong believer in euthanizing those with terminal illnesses, but more along the lines of, I don't know, I guess, advocacy is the right word."

"Not sure I understand."

"He wanted to change people's minds about it. Try to explain the positive side of it."

"And you believe he acquired his beliefs while his father was sick."

"Yes. Before that, he never mentioned it."

"While you worked together, was there anything involving him that you considered unusual?"

"What do you mean by that?"

"Were there any incidents or situations involving him where someone might have been hurt or put in danger? Anything that cast suspicion on him?"

Bullard slid his empty plate to the side and leaned in. "I didn't think much of it when it happened, but his father was near the end, and he said his mother was going to call hospice in. He was going to be brought home, and that they expected him to last two to three weeks. But a day later he passed away."

"You think Vape had something to do with speeding up the death?"

He shrugged. "Like I said, it never hit me until he started getting vocal about euthanasia. But why not?"

Why not indeed? It was logical. If you saw someone you loved suffering, you'd want to intervene somehow. But killing your father?

"Anything else?"

"I mean, this was a long time ago. We were in school, and

one Friday night we drank like college kids do and were ossified. He starts telling me that when he was in high school he hit some kid with his car and took off. He didn't say it, but I got the feeling the kid died."

"Where was this?"

"Cape Coral."

"And Vape was in high school at the time?"

"That's what he said."

"Whose car was he driving?"

"I'm pretty sure it was his parents'."

There was nothing concrete in what Bullard said about Vape's father or the hit-and-run that I could work with. We'd never find out the truth concerning the speed of his dad's death, but we could check with Lee County on a vehicular homicide.

38

AFTER CASHING IN A COUPLE OF FAVORS WITH THE LEE County Sheriff's Office, I ran the possibilities and their impact on the case.

It was possible that Vape killed a kid. If so, the crime was decades old, and at the time, Vape was a minor himself. He may have panicked and ran rather than report it. It wasn't excusable but entirely plausible.

If true, what interested me was what the episode proved. To me it was evidence that Vape was able to suppress his conscious. He went on with his life as if nothing had happened. It was a callous reaction, one that would serve useful if he were a killer.

At the end of the day, killers, especially the serial type, were psychopaths. They shared the same flawed character traits. They had a lack of remorse, an impaired ability to empathize, were master manipulators, arrogant, and took big risks.

As I bounced a pencil on its eraser, an intern poked her head in my office.

"Excuse me, sir. This is for you." She held out a manila envelope.

"Thanks. Have a good one."

It was from the Financial Crimes Unit. I had asked FCU to uncover who the owners of Water's Edge were. I slipped out the document and did a double take. Two of the minority equity holders were none other than Fred Morley and Ryan Hall.

I was learning about the senior housing industry and had no idea how many players there were, nor what level of cross-ownership there was. But that aside, what were the odds that Morley and Hall would be involved? Water's Edge and Palm Shores were competitors. How could these guys own a piece of each of them?

Grabbing my jacket with one hand, I hit the light switch with the other before thinking of something. Tossing my jacket on the desk, I grabbed a file off Derrick's desk and picked up the phone.

"Water's Edge. How may I help you?"

"This is Detective Luca from the Collier Sheriff's Office. I'd like to speak to the administrator, please. That's Kelsy O'Hara, right?"

"Yes. But I'm sorry, she's attending a conference today. Can someone else help you?"

"I need to speak with someone who can provide information on the types of contracts some former residents had with you."

"Oh, I'll pass you to Antoinette."

"Administration. This is Antoinette."

I introduced myself and asked for the records.

"I'm sorry, but resident information is private. I don't think we can release that without an authorization."

"Please don't make me get a court order, ma'am."

"I'm sorry, sir, but I could lose my job, and I'm a single mother—"

"I understand. Can you answer a general question?"

"I'll try."

"Does Water's Edge have plans for its residents where they make a down payment or outright purchase to lower the ongoing fees they pay to you?"

"Yes, we offer choices."

"Okay. Take my number and have Ms. O'Hara call me immediately."

Slamming the phone down, I wondered why everything had to be so damn hard. Privacy was important, and I knew we needed rules, but we also needed information to keep people safe. The people I wanted info on were dead, for God's sake. Now I had to wait to find out if they had handed over sacks of money when moving in and how much they'd forfeited.

MORLEY'S blue sports jacket had brass buttons. Was it a new version of something they wore years ago, or did he have a closet full of pristine old clothing? He was always well manicured, but today I wasn't seeing sheen. It was slime.

He had the real estate section from Sunday's paper open to the estate home section. Was he close to selling Palm Shores and shopping for a new house?

"Before we get started, I'm going to want to speak to Ryan Hall when I'm finished with you."

"Ryan?"

"That's correct."

"I mean, of course, it's just surprising."

"Can you make sure he's available?"

"Sure." He picked up the phone and asked his secretary to track Hall down.

"Is it customary in the industry to invest in competitors?"

"Naturally, I can't speak for everyone, but it's something I'm not aware of."

"Really?"

"Yes. Is something the matter?"

"You own a piece of Water's Edge, don't you?"

He hesitated. "Yes. I fail to see why a private investment would interest the sheriff's office."

"Don't you think it contradicts what you stated about not investing in competitors?"

Morley smiled. "Water's Edge doesn't compete with us. Palm Shores is a one-of-a-kind property offering a unique, stylish way of life for those who appreciate the best."

This guy was a walking commercial. "So why the investment, then?"

"The senior marketplace is a large demographic. We cover the upper sliver of it, but there's money to be made in most areas, like the upper-middle segment, which Water's Edge services."

"What do you know about people dying there once they hit ninety."

His face whitened. "What are you referring to?"

"Surely you must be aware that a rash of residents died after turning ninety."

"I, I don't understand. I have no idea whatsoever about anything like that. I'm just an investor; I have no operational responsibilities."

It was time for a little fib. "That's not what we were told."

"Look, if they ask me my opinion on a matter, I'll offer it."

"So, you're an adviser to them as well as an investor."

"I wouldn't characterize it that way. People in the industry see what we've built here. They ask me questions. They don't have to follow my advice."

Stretching the truth yielded something, so I tugged it a little further. "We were told it was your idea for Water's Edge to offer the option to pay up front for lower monthly costs."

"I'm not sure it was my suggestion. I believe they were toying with the concept, and I wholeheartedly supported the initiative."

"Why do you believe it's such a good idea?"

"This industry is capital intensive. Building and maintaining these places is expensive and requires raising large amounts of money. If you can have the residents supply a portion of that cash, you don't have to borrow as much."

"You get it on both ends. They hand you a pile of cash when they move in, and when they die you don't give it all back."

"Residents who choose those plans enjoy savings on monthly costs."

"But it's a better deal for the facility."

"I wouldn't categorize it that way."

"If it wasn't, you wouldn't have told Water's Edge to go for it."

"This is a business, Detective. We offer a menu of plans to choose from."

"But the Palm Shores sales team pushes the down payment option."

"I don't believe that's an accurate assessment."

"You pay a higher sales commission on them. Don't you?"

"Yes."

"Why?"

He took a deep breath. "Because we can. Our borrowing

costs are just under seven percent. Even paying an extra two points to the salesperson, we still save five percent."

"Are you close to a sale on this place?"

His phone rang as he said, "We signed a nondisclosure agreement. All I can say is that we're in discussions at this time."

Morley answered the call. It was Ryan Hall. He was waiting in his office. I wrapped up the chat and headed a couple of doors down the hallway.

39

———————

RYAN HALL STOOD IN FRONT OF THE WINDOW, LOOKING AT the lake. The office reeked of cigarette smoke, and the rear of his sports jacket looked slept in. Ryan sniffled before turning around.

"You wanted to see me?"

He was distracted. "I take you away from something?"

"No, ah, yes, kind of. But it's okay; it really is. Take a seat. Can I get you something to drink? I'm crazy thirsty."

How had I thought he looked like Ryan Seacrest? "I'm okay."

He took a water bottle out of the small fridge by the couch and guzzled it. "You sure you don't want one?"

"No, thanks."

The bags under his eyes were big enough for a weekend outing. He might be sick. I said, "How's things going?"

He sat behind his desk. "Going? Great, yeah. We're humming along." He lowered his voice. "You know places like this, there's always an apartment to fill."

"Has management pressured you to get residents to agree to making payments in exchange for lower fees?"

He started rolling a pen back and forth with his fingers. "I wouldn't call it that."

"What would you call it?"

"Well, I mean, nobody interferes with me. Why would they? I keep this place full. I don't want to brag, but I'm good at what I do, and the clients like me. You know, I never had any complaints, not a single one, from anyone who moved in."

"You told me that you receive a higher commission on those deals. It seems natural to try and make as much as you can."

There was a slight tic above his right eye. "My job is to present the options and explain them. You make it seem like there's something wrong with selling those contracts. Ask around. I doubt you'll find anyone complaining about it."

"Tell me about Fred Morley. What is your relationship like?"

"It's pretty good, I think."

"That's it?"

He shrugged.

"Is he a difficult person to work for?"

"Everybody likes him. He can be hard at times."

"Can you provide an example?"

"I don't think I should be talking about any of that. I don't want to get in any more trouble."

"Trouble?"

"It's nothing. He was pissed at me; I took some time off. Sometimes I need to chill, you know?"

"You didn't tell anyone you were going to be out?"

"I forgot. It was kind of a last-minute thing. He'll get over it."

"It's come to our attention that you own a piece of Water's Edge."

His eyes darted away from mine. "It's nothing anymore. I got out of it last month."

"Why is that?"

"It wasn't making me much, and I have had things I wanted to do with the money."

"How does one go about selling something like that?"

"I had to discount it, not that it was a big deal. It was a small share. Morley took my piece; he got me in there in the first place."

"Fred Morley asked you to invest in Water's Edge?"

"He told me it was a good opportunity. He's done really well for himself, so I figured why not?"

"You bought it on his word?"

"Not a hundred percent. There's a lot of connections between the two places. I even helped out over there when they needed to close a couple of deals. A bunch of people who work at Palm Shores worked there too."

"Do some of the staff here still work there?"

"I don't think so. They had a period where they had trouble holding staff, and that's when we helped out. It's been at least two years since they recovered."

He reached for a tissue and blew his nose.

"You coming down with something or getting over it?"

"Can't seem to shake this."

"I assume Water's Edge also has a couple of options for potential residents, like the down payment one."

"They do, just like most places these days."

It was a troubling trend. If greed wasn't the motivating factor in this case, I was certain a homicide would land on my desk as a result of it. The numbers were too large, and the victims marginalized.

40

I stared into space, bothered that I couldn't tie Vape to a hit-and-run fatality. Why? I couldn't answer. It had no bearing on the Palm Shore case. Was I looking for confirmation that Vape had killed before and came up short?

The fact Lee County didn't have any unsolved hit-and-runs meant nothing. Vape could've hit a minor and thought he killed him, but the kid could've been lucky and suffered nothing more than a couple of bruises. Maybe he didn't even report it.

The important thing was Vape seemed to think he killed someone. Even though it was an accident, he left the scene and didn't give two damns about the teen. It was the twisted mindset of a murderer.

Derrick came in holding two cups of coffee and said, "You're in early."

I took one of the cups. "I'm taking the afternoon off. Mary Ann has that doctor's appointment at one. I wanted to get a couple of things done, but life isn't cooperating."

"Good luck with the doctor."

I sighed. "Thanks."

"What's going on?"

"Lee County can't find a record of an open vehicular homicide during the time in question."

"Maybe it didn't happen. The guy said Vape was drinking when he mentioned it. He could've been shooting his mouth off."

"I don't know. Why would he say something like that? You tell one of your only friends that you refused to help someone you hit by accident?"

"Maybe it wasn't an accident. Maybe he had a beef with the kid he hit."

"Telling someone you committed murder or attempted won't endear you to many people either."

"He felt guilty, wanted to unload it on someone. People confess all the time."

"Exactly. There had to be something to it. We have to dig deeper. Check court records for any suits, his work history, other people he went to school with. I don't care; check with his damn kindergarten teacher. There has to be something there."

"I'm on it." Coffee cup in hand, he headed to the door.

"Where you going? Finish your coffee first."

"I'm good; it's my second one. I'll see you later."

It was eight thirty. Why hadn't the administrator from Water's Edge called back? When a law enforcement officer asks you to call, you should show some respect. It's the least you could do. Was the disrespect for the police spreading down here?

I picked up and called her. She was in, making me angrier.

"Good morning, this is Kelsy O'Hara."

"This is Detective Luca from the Collier County Sheriff's Office."

"Oh, I saw you called. I was going to get back to you."

"I would hope so, ma'am. Police business should be a priority."

"I know, but I just came in. My daughter left her lunch home, and I had to run it over to the school."

"Know all about it. I have daughter as well; they have to come first. Look, the reason for my call is twofold. The first, I believe I know the answer to, concerns the type of contracts you offer to residents. Do you have people who pay a large fee upfront?"

"Yes. We have plans like those."

"And a portion of the money is not refundable?"

"That's correct. We use it to offset—"

"I'd like to know about three residents. They've passed on, but I'm interested to learn whether they had those types of agreements with Water's Edge."

She hesitated. "I'm not trying to give you a hard time, sir, but that information is private. I'd have to ask the families' permission before releasing anything like that."

"Forget it. I'll go to the families directly. Now, the second bit of information I need is a list of all your employees and the dates of service, going back the last five years."

"Five years? Is there something I need to be aware of?"

"I can't talk about an active investigation, but I can tell you Water's Edge is not the focus of attention. How soon can I have the list?"

DR. ALESSI GREETED us like old friends. With both of us bordering on frantic, it was exactly what we needed. He knew we were wound tight, and it was the first time he displayed the bedside manner we'd heard about.

He questioned Mary Ann on how she was feeling and how the last ten days had been before asking her about the pain she was experiencing. Fortunately, the shooting pains were less frequent and not as sharp.

Alessi examined her mouth first. He probed her jaw and teeth. My hope that it was dental related vanished as he moved to her eyes. Measuring their movement, Alessi asked how her vision was.

"It seems okay, but I find myself falling asleep after reading a chapter."

He said, "That makes two of us. I'm not detecting any loss in muscle movement. Let's check your balance and coordination. Stand up for a minute, please. Stand on your left foot. If you need to, steady yourself with the exam table."

Mary Ann lifted her right leg and faltered immediately. I couldn't believe my eyes.

"Okay. Try standing on your right leg. Good, good. Okay, you can sit back down. We're done."

I said, "What about the coordination tests?"

Dr. Alessi said, "They're not necessary."

Mary Ann's face darkened. She looked like she'd lost her best friend.

The doctor said, "It looks like you've had a flare-up. You mentioned experiencing facial pain for several days."

"Yes, for five days, but it's much better."

"That's a good sign. Normally these attacks last longer, sometimes a couple of weeks. Since this episode is receding so quickly, it appears to be minor in nature. I'm not minimizing the pain. I know it's difficult and frightening, but there is nothing to worry about."

"But we didn't expect her to get an attack so soon. You said that if the MS progressed, she might have attacks."

"I don't recall exactly what I said, but I can assure you

that every neurologist is aware of the unpredictability of multiple sclerosis. It's important to monitor all developments, so let me know if something crops up. In the meantime, I want you to remove as much stress as possible. Stress is a large factor in triggering attacks and in any progression of the disease. And make sure you get a solid eight hours of sleep."

I remembered the stress part and said, "Should she cut back on any activities?"

"Absolutely not. Mary Ann needs to exercise and stretch every day." He opened a drawer and took out a sheet of paper. "You should have these already. They're a couple of fundamental balance and core exercises. If it's not already, make it a part of your daily routine."

"Okay."

"I remember you stating you have a pool at home."

"Yes. We do."

"Are you swimming as I suggested?"

I had no memory of him mentioning that. Mary Ann shook her head.

"Make sure you swim laps each day. It's one of the best things you can do for yourself. That and a long walk every day."

Had he really told us this before? Were we zoned out with the seriousness of her diagnosis and missed this important information?

41

Holding hands, we came out of the doctor's office into the sunshine. The sun was high in a cloudless sky. Walking to the Cherokee, I said, "Everything is going to be okay."

"You really think so?"

"I know so. Look, neither of us expected a flare-up so soon. Maybe he said something about it, but it doesn't matter. You had one, but it was a little one. You're not feeling any pain, right?"

"No. Not since this morning."

"You gotta start exercising regularly."

"I was doing some, but I guess I have to ramp it up."

We climbed into the SUV, and pulling away, I said, "This is going to be good."

"What do you mean?"

"We'll make it a family thing, swimming together. It'll be good for Jessie. She'll learn the importance of exercising, and maybe I'll even get my physique back. I think I left it in high school somewhere."

"I can hardly swim. I hate it."

"You'll get better. Just start with a couple of laps a day. I'll get you a kickboard so you don't drown, okay?"

"Very funny. You're the one who almost drowned, not me."

She was right. I had swum off the beach toward a rock outcropping about a mile off a Mexican beach. More than halfway out, a wave slapped into my mouth, and I swallowed a cupful of saltwater. It was enough to fluster me. Instead of keeping my head, I began to panic, thrashing around in the water. There wasn't a person or boat around. I was completely alone. Out of nowhere, I realized I was going to drown, and no one would know what was happening until it was too late.

As a wave submerged my head, the instinct to survive kicked into gear, and the voice in my head moved from terror to instruction. I started to swim away from the shore to the closer rock formation. I made it to the outcropping and rested. I never gave a thought to staying there to be rescued before swimming back.

Though I pushed through and survived, the experience changed me. It was my first brush with vulnerability, and I didn't like it. I never mentioned the episode to anyone until I told Mary Ann after we got engaged.

I swallowed what I wanted to say and said, "I'll get all of us swimmies. We should make a schedule. Break it up. Maybe I can come home at lunch and swim with you, and then after dinner we'll take a walk as a family. Maybe Jessie can ride her bike as we walk."

"Come on, Frank. Be realistic. I'll do the swimming when Jessica is at school, and we'll walk at night."

"I can do it with you."

"It's okay. There's no need to come home in the middle of the day."

MY RIGHT SHOULDER was bothering me. Last night I had swum forty-two laps in our thirty-foot pool. You couldn't call that showing off. I was trying to motivate Mary Ann.

Entering the office, I held a coffee in my left hand.

Derrick had a puzzled look on his face. Were his observation skills better than mine? "Morning. How'd it go at the doctor's?"

"It was an MS attack."

"Oh, geez. She going to be all right?"

"Yeah, she rebounded already." I tossed what was left of my coffee in the trash and picked up the Starbucks my partner got me.

"Anything we can do to help?"

Powering up my desktop, I said, "We're okay, thanks. Apparently these things come out of nowhere but they go away. Or at least that's what we're hoping."

"If there's anything, and I mean anything, you know you can count on us."

"I know. Thanks, pal."

"Something the matter with your arm?"

Opening my email box, I said, "Nah, shoulder is a little stiff, must have slept on it wrong."

"Lynn has a chiropractor she swears by. Since she's been pregnant, her back has been killing her, and she hasn't been able to do anything. It's terrible. So now she goes twice a week to him. It seems to be helping."

"That's good." As I went down the list of emails, I couldn't help thinking how relative everything was. In his house, a backache from pregnancy was considered a catastrophe, while in mine, we were dealing with a true crisis.

I opened an attachment from Kelsy O'Hara. The pdf had

five pages. I hit print and scrolled down the list. It was organized by date, starting with the current employees of Water's
Edge. The first two pages were unremarkable.

Midway down page three, I said, "Are you kidding me?"

"What's the matter?"

"Ben Porter worked at Water's Edge when those ninety-
year-olds died."

"Oh my God. This is crazy. Why would he do it?"

"I don't know. Maybe he's getting paid by Morley."

"Could be. What about some voodoo connection?"

"I don't think so."

"What if it's racial? All the victims were white."

It was something I hadn't considered. It wasn't that I
didn't think these types of biases didn't exist. When they did,
there were usually signs of the hatred. Evil-looking eyes
aside, Porter didn't fill the hate crime profile. "I doubt it, but
we'll have to take a look."

"Let me cross-check the dates. Make sure Porter was
working on the dates of the deaths."

"Exactly. Did you cross-check Vape already?"

He hung his head. "Not yet."

Instead of beating him up on a fundamental oversight, I
said, "Do them together, then."

"If you think Porter is mixed up with Morley, we should
get financial records to see if any money is passing between
them."

"I wanted to wait on any subpoenas. Put them all in one
request. Get Palm Shores, maybe even Water's Edge, along
with personals on Morley and Porter."

"Sounds like a plan." He took the papers off the printer
and made a copy. "I'm going to go down to Water's Edge."

"Before you go, give me the family contact info on the
three deaths."

42

MY CONFIDENCE GREW THAT THE SAME PERSON OR PERSONS who killed Bill Coby and Charles Martin in Palm Shores had done so out of greed. Calls to two Water's Edge families had confirmed that their loved ones, who died after turning ninety, had entered into contracts requiring large deposits.

Though the families considered it a strategy to offset costs, my belief that it was a scheme to defraud seniors was firming. It was also ramping up the possibility of a conspiracy with Morley at the helm.

Was he paying Porter to kill with the money he'd make? Was there any way Vape could be involved? I wondered whether the two men could have forged an alliance with such different goals.

I dialed a number for the family of one of the ninety-year-olds and a woman answered.

"Hello?"

"Good day, ma'am, I'm Detective Luca with the Collier Sheriff's Office."

"The sheriff?"

"Yes, ma'am. We're looking into a situation at Water's Edge, where your mother resided."

"Oh. How can I help you?"

"We trying to determine the type of arrangement that led to her moving there."

"She was having difficulty taking care of herself, and me and my sister, we work, and it was just getting too much for us—"

"I understand. I'm interested to know what type of contract she signed. Did she make a down payment before moving to get lower fees or anything like that?"

"Down payment? Momma didn't have much, otherwise we could have had someone come to her apartment. Me and sis couldn't help much; we both have three kids and—"

"To be clear, no money was paid to Water's Edge before she moved in?"

"Well, she had to pay the first two months, I think it was, and me and sis had to sign that if Momma didn't pay, we'd have to make good for it. We weren't worried, 'cause she had her Social Security and a pension from my dad; he worked on the railroad, to cover it."

"And you're certain no money changed hands?"

"Yep, she didn't have it, and neither did we. All Momma had was what she got each month. Never owned a house, which was a big mistake. I keep telling my sis that she has to buy something, but now with the kids—"

"Can you give me your sister's contact information?"

I jotted down the info and said, "Thank you, ma'am. I've got to go."

Dialing the dead woman's other daughter, I tried to understand what I was just told. It didn't jibe with the greed theory. Was she wrong or misinformed? I'd check with the sister to be sure.

WHERE WAS DERRICK? I needed to know what he found out. Rain pelted the window as I punched his number in.

"What did you get from them?"

"I'm pulling into the parking lot. I'll be in in a minute."

Derrick's shirt was peppered with wet spots. "Man, it just started coming down in buckets."

"We need it. Last month we had under an inch of rain."

"Really?"

"Uh-huh. What did you find out?"

He opened his notebook. "It's kind of crazy. You'll never guess what they told me."

"Enlighten me, then."

"Vape and Porter were at Water's Edge for two of the deaths." He looked at his notes. "Both of them were there for the Fina woman, and Vape was visiting his mother when Mrs. Ramirez died, but Porter was off that day. When Mrs. Olsen died, Vape was in Tampa at a convention, but Porter was working."

"Ramirez is the only one who didn't hand over any cash."

"That makes sense if it's Porter and Morley working together. There was no money to be gained by murdering her."

"If she was killed, and it's a big if, it could have been Vape."

"Man, this is confusing."

"Let's run through this." I grabbed a marker and wrote the names of the dead. "We have a total of five dead, that we know of. Colby and Martin at Palm Shores. They're the only two we know for certain were murdered."

"Vape and Porter were both there the nights they were poisoned."

"And there was a lot of money sucked up by Palm Shores when they died." A crack of thunder sounded as I drew dollar signs next to their names.

"A contract kill, executed by Porter, allowing Morley to enrich himself. Or Vape exercising his euthanasia beliefs."

"Those are the main themes at the moment. Now, at Water's Edge we have three suspicious deaths. Two of which could be for the money but not the third. Complicating it, assuming the Porter-Morley alliance, Porter wasn't there for one of them."

"Maybe Morley used someone else for the other murder."

Drawing question marks next to the other names, I said, "Or it's possible one or all of the Water's Edge deaths were natural and we're chasing smoke."

"Maybe not all of them. Let's say there was no foul play with Ramirez . . . oh, Porter was there for only one of the others then."

"True, but what if it was Vape? He was there for two of the three, and money isn't a motivator. The third death could have been natural."

"That's plausible. But so is Porter killing just one of them. The others could have died of old age. Let's not forget they were ninety."

"True. So, at this point the Water's Edge info gets us nowhere if we can't expound upon it. We know Porter was at Palm Shores, not only for the poisonings, but also for a couple of weird coincidences, and you know how I feel about coincidences."

"Put the focus on him?"

"And Vape. We have to two-prong this. We have greed on one side and a belief in euthanasia on the other."

"But these aren't mercy killings. These poor people were in good health."

"I know it doesn't jibe with the conventional viewpoint. Even though it impacted Vape to see his father suffer, something else might be going on in his head. A big part of this job is getting inside the mind of a killer. I'm not saying he is, but Vape might be seeking some twisted sense of revenge."

"Revenge? For what?"

"He could feel he lost his father too early."

"And he's jealous, so he kills?"

"It's not rational to you and me, but all I'm saying is we have to consider every possibility until we're able to discount them."

"I got you."

"Are we missing any links between the victims and any possible ones?"

"You mean did they know each other?"

"There is no evidence they did. I'm talking about a profile."

"They're all seniors; not all of them had money though. They're all Caucasian."

"No, some were Hispanic." As I paged through the murder book, I saw Galena Vuvich's name and remembered what she said about Porter hating her because she was an Orthodox Christian. "I know Bill Coby was Catholic. What about the others?"

43

———

I DIDN'T KNOW WHAT, IF ANYTHING, IT MEANT THAT ALL THE victims were Catholic. Some were devout and others were "holiday Catholics," only going to Mass on Christmas and Easter. Could Porter have some personal beef with the religion and wanted to eliminate followers?

It seemed like a long shot. Why kill the older faithful? Why not target younger practitioners? It didn't make sense, but neither did any of the indiscriminate killings taking place around the world in the name of religion.

There was a lot to ask Porter about, and it was time to do it. Driving south on Tamiami Trail, I debated whether to ask for a warrant to view Porter's financial records. The problem was you couldn't put the TV on without hearing about how we were losing our privacy.

It was a concern. Civil liberty organizations were beating up social media outfits but had used the uproar to also attack law enforcement on overreaching. As a result, Chester wanted the department to consolidate its requests. I knew what he was up to. The politician in him wanted to trot out figures showing a decline in subpoenas issued.

I also knew that judges, despite their claim to be above the fray, were requiring more evidence before signing off on a search. At this point, I felt I had enough evidence to ask for Palm Shores, Morley, and Porter's records but didn't have a good enough basis to request Water's Edge.

Either way, the scope of the records I wanted would take days to sort through. I didn't have much belief in the religion angle, but it made sense to wait until I ran it down before burying myself in numbers.

I saw her fireplug shape through the glass entrance. Galena Vuvich was in someone's face again. As the doors slid open, I heard the woman she was speaking with say, "No, that's not true." Vuvich told her to make sure it never happened again and turned my way.

She waved at me, and I beckoned with my hand.

"Having a little trouble today?"

"Galena can take care of herself."

"I'm sure you can. You have a minute?"

"For you, my George Clooney, anything."

"Let's step outside."

She smiled. "Galena is going on date?"

"You had said that Ben Porter didn't like you because you were an Orthodox Catholic. Why do you believe that?"

"He don't like us. He blames Catholics for something about his father, when he die."

"Did he tell you that?"

"Not him. But there used to be woman; she was from Jamaica too. She used to work in dining room. She says Porter tell her his father can't rest in peace because of Catholics."

"He disliked all Catholics?"

"Yes, he smiles to everyone, but behind is evil."

I thanked her and went to the reception area trying to

understand the meaning, if any, to what I had just heard. Vuvich was devout and belonged to a sector of Catholicism that was relatively small in America.

I watched Vuvich play cards with her client. I wondered if she was defensive about her beliefs. Then Morley came in the building leading a small group. He told them, "You've seen our great room already; let's head over to the movie theater. It's something special."

He hesitated when he saw me, smiled, and moved on.

The receptionist said, "How are you today?"

"Good. Boy, it must be busy if Morley's showing apartments."

She shook her head. "Not really. Ryan's missing in action. Again."

"He okay?"

"Probably, but who knows? He's not answering his phone."

"You want me to send a car over and make sure everything is all right?"

"Nah, I'm sure it's just Ryan being Ryan."

"Okay, I forgot; he told me where he lives, but I forgot."

"He has an apartment in Le Mer by Venetian Village."

Le Mer was an expensive place to call home. "Nice. If you want us to check things out, let me know. Can you page Ben Porter?"

"Be my pleasure."

A minute later, Porter sidled up to me. It bothered me that I hadn't heard him approach. It was his show of stealthiness that heightened my suspicions.

"You want me?"

"Yes. Let's go into the café."

My stomach gnawed. I don't know if it was the smell of

coffee or the plate of chocolate cookies. I closed the French doors behind us and sat at a newspaper-covered table.

"I know you're working, so I'll get right to it. Tell me about your time working at Water's Edge."

"A couple of years ago I needed money and took a part-time job there."

"How many days a week?"

"One, maybe two times a week."

He was lying. Unless they were paying him like a doctor, the payroll amounts on state records translated to three or four days' pay. "How did you find the job?"

"Oh, I don't know. It was a long time ago."

"Did you know that Fred Morley owned a part of Water's Edge?"

The slightest of hesitations. "I heard, but I don't know if it was before or after I started working there."

"Did he tell you about the opening?"

"I don't think so."

That was a yes in my book, meaning Morley positioned him there. "You practice voodoo, don't you?"

"It's not voodoo. It's voudon."

"Sorry, I understand you don't care much for Catholics."

He shrugged.

"Why is that?"

"Nothing special."

"It's because of your father and his death, isn't it?"

"They don't understand. They make only two percent of the population, but they stopped us from preparing a proper resting place."

"And how did they do that?"

"They don't allow Nine Night."

"Tell me what that is. Maybe I can help."

"It's too late."

"Explain Nine Night."

"The journey to the afterworld takes nine days after you die. Ghosts and evil spirits linger after death for nine days. On the ninth night, we have what you call a wake, to celebrate them leaving. It's the only way to get eternal peace in the next life. Now my father is haunted by duppies for eternity."

"Duppies?"

"Evil spirits."

"Why couldn't you hold the service?"

"The Catholics convinced my mother that a body must be buried quickly and that Nine Night is nothing but an excuse for people to drink and dance."

"I'm sorry you were unable to have the funeral you wanted for your father. It must have made you upset."

He nodded slowly. The look in his eyes made me think about the evil Vuvich had seen.

"Let me ask you about Water's Edge. While you were there, three people died in a short time frame. What was unusual was that they all had just turned ninety. What can you tell me about that?"

He averted his eyes. "I don't know about that."

"Really. I understand that part of your responsibilities there was to give a thorough cleaning when someone died or moved. Packing up their personal belongings and readying the apartment for a new resident. Wasn't it?"

"Uh-huh."

"All three of the residents were Catholic, but you knew that, didn't you?"

"Most everyone down here is."

"Not true. There are more Protestants by far."

He smiled. "Maybe that's why I like it here."

"Did you have anything to do with the deaths of anyone

in Water's Edge?"

"These people are old, man. They pass to another world, that's all. Don't make a big deal of it. I got to get back to work, man."

44

———

Sheriff Chester eyed me wearily as I was shown into his office. Anytime I requested a meeting he'd become concerned I'd bring something to worry about.

"Take a seat, Frank."

"Thank you, sir."

"I've been meaning to ask, how's Mary Ann doing?"

"She's doing fine, sir."

"Excellent, that's good to hear. When she's ready to return to duty, let me know."

There was no way she was coming back to the stress of being an officer. "I will, sir."

"What's on your mind?"

"As was mentioned in the report, we have three suspicious deaths at Water's Edge—"

"What makes them suspect?"

"All the deaths occurred within a two-week period, and each one of them had turned ninety within days of passing."

"Ninety? I'd sign up for that."

"I hear you, but all were in excellent health."

"I trust you have more than that."

"Yes. Two people of interest in the Palm Shores homicides have ties to Water's Edge. One worked there, and the other is a partner. And another person we're looking into, his mother was a resident at Water's Edge before moving to Palm Shores."

"Incestuous."

"It is. What we need to confirm or dismiss is whether foul play was involved. Unfortunately, the only way to determine if these cases are related is an autopsy."

Chester's eyes rolled. "You want to exhume three bodies? Have you lost your mind?"

"Not three, sir—"

"These people were ninety. There's no way the county is going to get involved in this. Forget it."

"I understand, sir, but what if we can get the families to do it, like we did with Coby?"

"They have their rights, but I won't allow my department to prod grieving families into something like this."

"Would you allow me to approach one family about the possibility?"

As the sheriff steepled his fingers, I added, "It would go a long way in helping to close the case."

"I don't like this, and I don't want anyone babbling to the damn press about it. I'll let you do it, but keep it discreet."

I rose before he could change his mind. "Thank you, sir."

***

ENTERING THE OFFICE, I flashed a smile and thumbs-up to Derrick.

"The sheriff agreed?"

"Not exactly. He said we can approach one of the families to see if they'll do it privately."

"Which one?"

"At this point, we'd get information if there was a homicide from any of them, but I'm leaning toward focusing on Porter."

"Really? What about Vape?"

"I know, but there's just too much noise surrounding Porter. We need to see if Olsen was poisoned. If she was, we know it was probably Porter."

"I don't know. Vape's mother was there, and his euthanasia fixation is awful hard to set aside."

"We have to pick one, and Porter feels right to me."

"Okay, but do you really think the family is going to go for it?"

"I hope so. No doubt it's an emotional thing to go through."

"I'll bet. And it's expensive too. It'll probably run them a couple of thousand dollars. I don't know why they'd ever agree to do it."

"Life insurance. If the Olsen woman was murdered, it's considered accidental, and the beneficiaries of her life insurance would get two to three times whatever they got so far."

"That's a good angle. I didn't think of it that way."

"And for that, you get to do the ask. Let's go over the approach. We've got to strike the right chord, something about the good it would do, adding more meaning to her life, that sort of thing, and then, with that percolating, you sneak in the possible windfall they'd get."

DERRICK'S WARNING about Vape and his euthanasia obsession made me hedge the bet. Pulling into the college where Vape taught, I caught sight of him walking into the same lot where I was headed. My instincts took over. I made a quick right and headed away, down a row of parked cars.

Vape got into his Prius and backed out of a space. After he exited, I followed him. He turned right onto Collier Boulevard. I stayed a handful of car lengths behind. I didn't know what there was to gain, but as long as I kept my distance, all I had to lose was a little time.

At the Tamiami Trail intersection, he made another right. Vape drove for a couple of miles before putting his directional on. He slowed down and made a right. Vape was going to Tuscany Villa. It was another assisted living place. What the hell was he doing there?

I passed the entrance and backtracked, trying to determine the odds he was going to claim another victim. Pulling into the driveway of the rose-colored complex, I found a spot, deep in the lot, with a view of the front doors.

Only three reasons came to mind for why Vape could be here: he could be visiting someone; he could be scouting another place for his mother to live, or he could be up to no good. It was the middle of the day. If he was going to murder, it wouldn't follow the killer's MO.

The only thing I could do without embarrassing myself and putting Vape on alert was leave. I'd make discreet inquiries to find out what he was doing there.

"IT'S a beautiful day at Tuscany Villa. How can I help you?"

First thing that ran through my head was whether she would say that if someone had died yesterday.

"Hi, this is Detective Luca from the sheriff's office."

"Oh, what can we do for you, sir?"

"I'm sure you've heard about what happened at Palm Shores."

"Oh my God. It's so sad."

"As a result, we're keeping in touch with many places, checking in with them."

"That's a good idea."

"Just part of our duty, ma'am. Now, can you tell me whether anyone in your complex passed away yesterday?"

"No, not that I'm aware of."

"That's always good."

"It sure is."

"Oh, by the way, yesterday I was driving by and thought I saw someone I knew going into your building. Were you working yesterday afternoon?"

"Yes. I was here. Who do you think it might have been?"

"My buddy's name is Brian Vape."

"Oh, Brian comes in from time to time. He's a volunteer. He helps train the technicians doing our X-rays."

"Oh. I think he told me about that. How long has he been doing that?"

"I don't know. He was coming here when I started, and that was a year and a half ago."

After thanking her, I hung up, and leaned back in my chair. Was Vape even cleverer than I thought? It was a perfect way to gain access to the elderly in a role that bestowed unearned trust on him.

A feeling of helplessness began creeping up my stomach. If he was the killer, how could we even begin to find people like Vape in the future? As my mood sank, the phone rang.

"Hey, Derrick, what's going on?"

"The Olsen son is on board. He even called his sister and she agreed."

I wondered if it was a sense of duty or the money that swayed them, but I knew the answer. Before hanging up, I filled Derrick in on Vape's volunteer work.

45

———

Waiting for Derrick to arrive, I stood before the whiteboard, switching my focus between pictures of Vape and Porter. Porter's eyes weren't evil, as Vuvich claimed, but I was getting something from them. They had a strange, weird look.

The word otherworldly popped into my mind, but I was clearheaded, realizing it was because he practiced a religion that had been fictionalized by Hollywood. What was true about his beliefs? I sat down and starting Googling for answers.

I started with Nine Night. All along, we had followed the possibility Porter was motivated to kill for money. We needed to know if an issue with a tradition could tip him into revenge killing. The internet had no shortage of information on Jamaican burial practices.

As Porter said, traditional beliefs held that a body couldn't be buried until nine days after death. Their firmly held supposition was that the extended time was needed to allow bad ghosts, or duppies, to leave the body. If the body was prematurely buried, then the duppies would wreak havoc on the neighborhood and prevent the dead from achieving a peaceful state. The body would suffer under a permanent spell.

Reading a section on trying to cleanse the spell, I came across Obeah, a form of witchcraft from West Africa that took root in Jamaica. Catholics considered the practice satanic, and it was no longer legal in Jamaica, though some still practiced it.

When Derrick walked in, I said, "It's hard to believe that people like Porter still believe in evil spirits, potions, and spells."

"It's not witchcraft anymore, it's called a diverse set of beliefs."

"Holy shit."

"What?"

"It says here that way back, many white Jamaicans accused Obeah believers of poisoning people. They claimed the potions they used to get rid of a ghost were actually deadly. Come here, look at this."

I read the passage out loud, "'Doctor's investigating several deaths found the presence of arsenic as one of the powders used by the Obeahmen. These findings led to a movement that made Obeah illegal to practice.'"

Derrick said, "Using a drug to overdose is just another version of poisoning."

"No doubt. Porter might have put his own twist on it."

"Porter said he blamed Catholics for preventing the nine funeral thing. Do you think he's targeting them for revenge?"

"Could be, or maybe it's a combination including money. Hey, is Morley Catholic? If Porter doesn't like them, I can't see him conspiring with one."

"How we going to find out?"

"Ask him. He wants to tell us, fine. If not, I'll get the answer from somebody."

I picked up the phone and called Palm Shores.

"Mr. Morley, this is Detective Luca."

"How are you today?"

"Good. I have a couple of questions for you."

"I'm afraid it isn't a good time. I'm just about to go into a meeting."

"This won't take long."

Morley sighed heavily. "If you must. But please keep it short."

"What is your religious persuasion?"

"That's an odd question."

"You don't have to answer it if you feel it's a private matter."

"I'm a Methodist."

"Your entire life?"

"Yes. My parents were as well."

"Thank you for sharing that. Now, I'm curious to understand how Ben Porter came to be employed at Water's Edge. Did you have something to do with that?"

"That was years ago. I don't remember doing anything. Keep in mind, I'm an investor and have no operational responsibilities or influence."

"Most companies want to keep their investors happy, don't they?"

"Sometimes."

"And in your particular case, they've already taken your advice, offering a down payment model to residents."

"They were moving in that direction anyway; it simply made sense for them. My opinion didn't move the needle."

That was bullshit, and we both knew it. "Did you ask them to hire Ben Porter?"

"No."

"Did you tell Mr. Porter to apply for employment there?"

"That was several years ago. I really don't recall."

"Are you sure? Our sources seem to believe you did."

"It's altogether possible. I may have mentioned something in passing. But I can't be sure."

"And why would you have recommended that to him?"

"Why? He was looking for a job, that's why."

"Does Mr. Porter do a good job at Palm Shores?"

"Yes. We hire only the best."

"Is it customary for an employer to suggest to someone under his employ, someone who does a good job, to look for a job at a competitor?"

"They're not competitors. Palm Shores occupies a special space in the industry. There's simply no place offering the experience we do."

There was no doubt that Morley had something to do with Porter getting into Water's Edge. The question was whether he was simply helping someone or trying to place his assassin into an investment of his to juice returns.

I hung up and turned to Derrick, relaying the conversation to him. I said, "It's time to get a warrant for the financial records."

"I'll start it. We going for the whole enchilada, or you want to limit it?"

"We have to go wide. I want to see everything on Palm Shores, Water's Edge, Porter, and Morley. That way, we'll know if we're dealing with greed as a motivator."

"Okay, but what about Porter and the voodoo angle?"

"I'm not discounting it as a pure motive, but we haven't found anything in his past, and his father has been dead for eight years."

"If he kept his focus on the elderly it could have gone undetected."

"True, but sooner or later, things surface. Eight years is a long time. To me, if some kind of religious fanaticism is involved, then money might have pushed him over the edge."

"What if there's nothing in the records?"

"We focus like a laser on Vape and keep an eye on the Porter voodoo angle."

"I'll get this drafted and run it upstairs."

"The sooner the better. In the meantime, I'm going to stay on Vape, see what this volunteering thing is all about. He could be using it as a cover to gain access."

46

———

HEADING NORTH ON AIRPORT PULLING ROAD, I CROSSED over Pine Ridge and made a turn into a neighborhood of single-family homes. It was the first time I'd been in the area known as Tall Pines.

Passing houses in a mix of Old Florida and Mediterranean styles and price ranges, I turned onto Cypress Hollow Way. The roof of Vape's one-story home was covered with solar panels. Despite the abundant sunshine, there weren't many houses in Florida using solar power because electricity rates were reasonable.

I parked in back of his Prius and approached the front door as the next-door neighbor's black lab began barking. There was no doorbell, which I never understood. Wondering if there was a building code to have one and what type of person would remove one, I knocked on the door.

It took Vape under a minute to answer. He was wearing a T-shirt that read, "There is No Planet B," and he wasn't happy to see me.

"As I told you over the phone, I'm leaving to visit my mother."

"I'm aware; it won't take long. Can we do this inside?"

He stepped aside. "Sure."

The ranch home was warm and sparsely furnished. By the low ceilings and the home being much wider than it was deep, I estimated it was forty years old.

A brick wall, painted white, dominated the angled family room. It had the feel of one of those California houses in the sixties that I'd seen on TV. I looked through the sliders expecting to see a compost pile.

Vape motioned to a wooden dining table. "Let's sit here."

I eased onto a cushionless chair. "I see you've got solar on the roof. Is it worth doing?"

"Is it worth saving the planet?"

I nodded as he continued. "It's the least we can do. We're sucking up resources like we're the last generation to inhabit the Earth. It's selfish and greedy, if not criminal."

I went around shutting the lights in my house and got his point, but it wasn't against any law. "That's an interesting way to look at it."

"It's the only way. We're all connected, the people who've been here before us and those that will come in the future. We're inexorably linked. We have to share the resources we have and safeguard them for future generations."

"I don't know how bad the problem is. We seem to be making progress, especially with the younger generation. They're tuned into all this."

"They have to be. I mean, look at our parents' generation. They turned the water on and never gave a thought to running out of clean water or what kind of pollution comes from making power."

I shook my head. "Not in my house. My father used to complain that he wasn't a partner at Con Edison."

He smirked. "Do you know, when they started charging for water, usage went down? They need to do something like that with Medicare or it'll bankrupt us. Gobs of money is going into marginal drugs and procedures. Seniors don't give a damn; they feel they're entitled."

This was too close to home for me. "That's because they paid into the system."

Vape snorted. "The fact is, Medicare is spending almost four times the amount that they paid in. How long do you think we can keep that up?"

"Really? Four times? I didn't realize there was such a wide difference."

"Nobody does, or even cares. Medicaid is even worse. In Florida, Medicare is over thirty percent of our budget. A third of every dollar: it's nuts."

It was another statistic I hadn't known. "Don't we get money from the federal government?"

"We do; it's only ten percent, but where do the feds get their money from? Us."

"I guess taxes are going to go up, again."

"It would have to go crazy high or they'd have to do something about what's being spent in the final year of someone's life. Do you know that alone sucks up about thirty percent of what Medicare spends each year?"

"I knew that, but what are they going to do? Euthanize people?"

"Look, I'm sorry we got off on a tangent, but I've got to get going. What did you want to ask me?"

He avoided my setup question. Vape was too smart to say something he'd regret later. "I understand that you also work at Tuscany Villa."

"It's pro bono. I'm a volunteer and don't get paid."

"What do you do for them?"

"Most places don't have a radiologist on staff. It's just too expensive, so they employ radiology technicians, X-ray techs, to handle their medical imaging. First and foremost, I make sure they understand the risks of exposure and go over the precautions they must exercise. It's dangerous work. Then I make sure they understand what to look for and who to alert if they believe there might be an area of concern."

"Do you volunteer anywhere else?"

"Yes, a week doesn't go by that I don't conduct training somewhere."

"Where else do you do this?"

"Barrington, Terracina, Lely Palms, Brookdale, Moorings Park, and Harbor Chase."

My stomach dropped further with each name I jotted down. "That seems like a lot of volunteering. Where do you find the time to do all that?"

"The college is good about it, and they should be. It helps attract students to their radiology program."

"And how long have you been going to all these places?"

"Five or six years. Look, I'm sorry, but I've got to go. Mom is expecting me, and if I'm late, she gets out of sorts."

Leaving, I tried to process what I'd learned. The idea that we had to look for foul play at the six facilities he volunteered at was depressing. The real question involved his motivation for acting like the Mother Teresa of radiology.

Was Vape doing his part in some whacky belief he needed to save Medicare from bankruptcy, or was he just paying it forward, lending his medical expertise to the next generation?

Stopped at a light on Pine Ridge Road, I batted around whether Vape was simply an unselfish person, concerned about the planet and his fellow man, or a calculating psychopath, taking his belief in euthanasia to a deadly degree.

As the light turned green, my cell rang. It was Derrick. He wanted to let me know we'd have the financial records tomorrow.

47

———

The first thumb drive arrived from JP Morgan Chase. It was the bank that Palm Shores used, and my guess that Morley also used it was right. Most business owners bank with the same institution personally. The bulk of what we wanted to look through was in our hands.

We had determined, through Palm Shores' payroll records, that Porter used Bank of America. They had promised to comply with the warrant by the end of tomorrow, at the latest. I palmed the flash drive not knowing what to expect.

I inserted the drive, hoping some kind of a sort function was possible. A menu popped open. I chose the Palm Shores account, selected 2019 and transaction details. A dialog box appeared, warning the file was read only. I hit okay and an impossibly long Excel file opened.

Before everything became digital, it took considerable time and effort for financial institutions to comply with a warrant. Time wasn't the only downside, as I remembered receiving reams of documents when we made a request. In some cases, it took weeks to comb through it to find anything worth digging further into. The move to microfiche was an improvement but nothing like the spreadsheet I was staring at.

Excel and I weren't the closest of friends. I hoped using the simple find and sort functions would make me look like a techie. I typed Porter into the find slot. A long list of transactions appeared.

The first eight were consistent amounts paid twice a month to Porter. They were payroll transactions. The next one was a round number: two thousand dollars. It was paid on February 4, 2019. I printed the page it appeared on and continued my search.

A dozen more payroll checks, and the year was over. I checked 2018 and 2017, but there was nothing but payroll checks. It made sense. Morley was no fool. If he was paying Porter to kill, he wouldn't have the company pay for it. He probably didn't even write a check from his account either.

Checking payments to Morley revealed a hodgepodge of checks. Smaller amounts were probably expense reimbursements, but there were steady monthly checks in the amount of thirty thousand dollars and large, quarterly ones in varying amounts, none under forty grand.

He was drawing thirty grand a month, and it looked like profit sharing, depending upon the results. Morley was raking it in. The question was whether it was based upon sound business practices or foul play.

If the business had made more money by keeping a deceased's down payment, it could be legitimate. We'd need more to prove there was a connection between the deaths and the larger bonuses.

Navigating back to the menu, I opened up the transactions on Morley's personal account. It was a dramatically smaller file, but I still searched for anything paid to Porter. Just one line item appeared. It was a ten-thousand-dollar payment made to Porter in November of 2018. Was this the smoking gun we were looking for, or was there an explanation for such an off-the-book's payment to an employee?

I printed the page and tried again to be sure the find function was working properly. There didn't seem to be any other payments to Porter.

Wondering whether he had made a payment to a third party, I decided to go line by line through the fifteen pages of records.

Morley made a lot of money and spent much of it. Many of the recipients were business names I recognized. He also seemed to be generous, writing regular checks to the Immokalee Foundation and Wounded Warriors. Wondering if his philanthropy was a cover, I paged down.

I did a double take. There was a twenty-thousand-dollar payment to Ryan Hall. It was just two months ago, so it couldn't be for the Water's Edge stake. After printing the page, I typed Hall into the find bar. There was nothing else.

We had a couple of payments that demanded an explanation, especially the Morley to Porter check for ten grand. I wanted to wait on the Bank of America paperwork before asking questions. There was no use alerting anyone, giving them time to try and cover things up.

I sent a text to Derrick to let him know I had to take Mary Ann to the doctor's and that I'd see him in the morning.

IT WAS a little after ten when I walked into the office. Derrick looked over his monitor. "Morning. Is everything all right?"

"Yeah. Just running late."

"You sure? Nothing going on with Mary Ann or anything?"

"She's fine; it was a routine visit. We had the water heater replaced this morning. I didn't want her to deal with it. I forgot to mention it."

"Okay, just wanted to be sure. Look, we got the Olsen autopsy report."

"That was fast. What do we have?"

He came around his desk holding a sheet of paper. "Nothing."

"What do you mean, nothing? Nothing in the blood panels?"

"Zippo."

As he handed me the document, I said, "They run a toxicology report?"

"Yep, nothing came up."

Collapsing into my chair, I read the report. "I can't believe it. You talk to the family?"

"Oh yeah. They weren't happy. Guess they might have been counting on a payday."

"I'll bet they were, but I feel terrible that we made them go through with all this."

"Me too. I told them we were sorry."

"I'll give them a call. Give me the son's number."

"Will do."

"I really thought we were going to find something that links all this."

"I thought so too. What now?"

"This doesn't clear Porter by any means, and Vape wasn't even there the day Olsen passed. I'd like to see if we can get one or both of the other families to go for an autopsy."

"You think the sheriff is going to agree to that?"

"Probably not, but I have to try." The phone started ringing as I said, "I'll go see him after I go through my emails."

Derrick answered and put the caller on hold. "Frank, it's a reporter from the *Daily News*. He wants to speak to you about the Olsen autopsy."

"How the hell did they find out about that?"

I picked up the phone. "This is Detective Luca."

"Good morning, Detective. Jonathan Pierce here, with the *Daily News*. I wanted to get your comments on a story we're running on the Olsen autopsy."

"What about it?"

"I understand you convinced the family to exhume the body of their beloved mother because you believed she was murdered."

"I wouldn't call it convincing them. We explained the situation and asked them for assistance."

"That's not what the son told us. He said he felt pressured by the police and was afraid not to cooperate. Can you comment?"

I wanted to tell him to go to hell but was able to restrain myself because I knew when the story broke Chester would be all over me, ending any hope of asking another family for help. "I stand by the characterization that we were seeking assistance and that we made it clear it was completely voluntary."

"What made you believe this woman was murdered? Do you have proof of any kind?"

"I can't comment on an active investigation."

We played ping-pong for another couple of minutes before I begged off the call. I slammed the receiver down.

"Forget about giving me the son's number, and find out where the hell the Bank of America records are."

48

Pushing away from my desk, I shook my head. "There's nothing particularly suspicious on the Bank of America records. A bunch of payroll checks to Porter and a fifteen thousand one every quarter to Morley."

"Probably some kind of dividend."

"There's got to be a trail somewhere. Maybe Morley has a relative or friend he's working this through, or Porter could be using his son or someone to wash the money."

"Could be. You going to question them?"

"Yeah, you have those copies I printed?"

"Me? I never had them."

"They're probably in the murder book."

Derrick leafed through it. "Nothing here. You sure you printed them?"

"Absolutely. Screw it. I'll reprint them."

Going through the JP Morgan Chase files, I found two of the three I was looking for, then I noticed a payment to Ryan Hall. It was dated the fifteenth of October and was for fourteen thousand dollars. I guess that's why he was driving a Bentley and I was piloting a Cherokee.

I popped his name in the find bar. A string of payments came up. Hall was receiving a check every two weeks for just under sixteen hundred. On top of that were larger checks, which must have been his commission checks.

"This kid Hall does damn good."

"My dad always said that sales is where to go to make real money."

"It's certainly not doing what we do."

I found the third check and printed it.

"I'll see you later."

As soon as Palm Shores' sliders opened, I saw Galena Vuvich. She was carrying a plate of cookies to a couple of residents playing cards. I checked in with reception, and before I could turn around, I heard squeaky footsteps approaching.

"Galena need to talk to you."

"Sure." I stepped toward the opposite side of the foyer. "What's going on?"

"You know what Vape man told Galena?"

Information was king, but why did people like to dangle what they knew, delaying the reveal moment? "No idea."

"He said, it's time for Mrs. Johnson to die. That to keep her alive was wasteful."

"How and when did he say this?"

"Yesterday. We are waiting to go into dining room, and Mrs. Johnson come back from hospital. She was in wheelchair being taken to her room. Galena feel bad for poor lady; she was bent over. Galena try to talk to her, you know, welcome her, but she doesn't say anything."

"Where was Mr. Vape when this was happening?"

"He was behind us, on line to go to eat. He says it was time for her to check out, that it was waste of money to keep her alive."

"Mr. Vape said that to you?"

"Yes. He is a bad man. I hear him many times talk the euthanasia."

"I appreciate the heads-up."

"Galena says to watch him. He is bad man."

"I'll do my best. If you see anything, don't hesitate to call me." She took the card I offered and said goodbye.

Watching her waddle away, the receptionist said her boss was ready to see me, shifting my thoughts from Vape to Morley.

Morley was on the phone and not happy. I stopped short of his doorway and heard him say, "Tell him to cut out the goddamn smoking. What, does he think he can show up after two days and stink this place up? Tell him I'm serious this time. I'm this close to firing him."

It was clear Morley was talking about Ryan Hall, probably to his HR person. I counted to ten before knocking on his open door.

Hunched over a document, Morley looked like he was pretending to be busy. He jumped to his feet.

"Come on in. Can we get you anything?"

"No thanks."

He smiled. "You change your mind, let me know."

Morley acted as if he was in a good mood.

"I'd like to ask you about a couple of checks that you and Palm Shores wrote."

"Checks?"

"Yes, we subpoenaed yours and Palm Shores' financial records."

His eyes widened. "That's confidential information. An invasion of privacy."

"It's a part of our investigation."

"Well, I object to the heavy-handed nature of your investigation."

"We understand your concerns, but your information is safe with us. Access is severely restricted in matters like this."

"I'm going to call my lawyer as soon as this conversation is over."

"You're free to do that at any time. We can provide a copy of the warrant to your counsel if you'd like."

He sighed.

"We found a payment from Palm Shores to Ben Porter in the amount of two thousand dollars. Why would he receive such a large sum?"

"When was this?"

"February fourth of this year."

"It probably was the bonus we distributed to our employees. They're the ones on the front lines, so to speak. Without them, we couldn't deliver such a high-quality experience."

"Every employee received one?"

"Yes, provided they were with us a minimum of six months."

"Everyone received two thousand dollars?"

"Well, no. The criteria are based on two principles; one that Palm Shores exceeds its budget, and then an employee's individual performance."

"What was the range of other bonuses?"

"I believe the baseline was a thousand."

"And you gave Ben Porter twice that amount. Why?"

"He earned it."

"You also wrote a personal check to Ben Porter for ten thousand dollars. What was the reason?"

He didn't ask for a date. Even rich people like Morley wouldn't forget a sum like that. "If I recall correctly, Mr. Porter was experiencing some financial pressure of some kind."

"You don't know specifically?"

"No."

"You hand him ten thousand dollars without asking for an explanation?"

"He has worked at Palm Shores for several years. It could have been for real estate or some family matter. I honestly don't recall."

He was lying. "Did you get anything in return for the ten thousand?"

"I don't understand."

That was more bullshit. "Did you ask Mr. Porter to do something for you? Was there a condition upon which you gave him the money?"

"I didn't give him the money; it was a loan."

"Has he paid any portion of it back?"

He hesitated. "Not yet, but there's no rush. I don't see the point about all this. I simply was trying to help an employee of the firm."

"How many other employees have you assisted monetarily?"

"It's not a practice I encourage, for obvious reasons, but there are times I step up when the need arises."

"Like with Ryan Hall?"

"We've done a few things together."

"Tell me about it."

"Ryan is an excellent salesperson, but he likes the finer

things in life, like his apartment, cars, and exotic vacations. Sometimes he gets in over his head."

"And you bail him out."

He shrugged.

"Like the twenty thousand you gave him?"

"He's not the best manager of money, but that's why he's in sales and not accounting, isn't it?"

"He makes what most people would consider to be a lot of money."

"True, but as soon as he receives his commission check, he starts spending as if he's going to get another the following week. He simply is unable to manage his financial affairs. So, I authorized accounting to pay his commissions monthly rather than every quarter to smooth things out for him. It seems to be working."

49

—————

After finishing with Morley, I went back to reception. Porter was supposed to meet me there but hadn't arrived yet. My pee-pee alarm went off. I'd been good about going every three hours like the doctors instructed, and with Mary Ann's troubles looming over the family, I wasn't going to take any chances.

I told the receptionist, "Ma'am, do me a favor. Tell Mr. Porter I'll be right back. I have to use the restroom."

There was a bathroom in the same hallway that led to Morley's office. I was about to push through the door when I saw Porter slip into his boss's office. They were getting their stories straight.

Sitting on the toilet, willing my revamped plumbing to release, I pondered the meaning of the two of them talking. It was a lazy slipup on their part. A call would have kept things out of the public eye.

Though Morley may have prearranged the meeting, it was likely he panicked when he learned we had the banking records. This could be the hairline crack we were looking for.

Drying my hands, I smiled at my reflection. I was looking

forward to seeing Porter squirm. The two of them thought they had their ducks all lined up, and I was going to ruin the party. It was one of the things I loved about my job.

Porter was talking with an aide. Approaching, I suggested we take a walk outside. I wanted him as comfortable as possible and still hadn't made up my mind whether to tell him I knew he and Morley had consulted.

I put my sunglasses on. The heat felt good. "Nice day."

"Yep."

We headed down a path of brown pavers that ran along tennis courts, ending at a lakeside gazebo. "This place doesn't pay that well, does it?"

"Same as others."

"They give out bonuses?"

"Uh-huh."

"You don't mind me asking, but how much you got this year?"

"I don't care none, it was two thousand."

Two women in tennis whites were practicing serving on the only active court as we walked by. "Pretty good. I guess they expect something in return."

"They got to pay the people; the job market for this kind of work is getting pretty good."

"You and Fred Morley are close friends."

"We get along."

"Got to be better than that, he gave you ten thousand dollars."

"He helped me when I was buying my condo."

"I thought your son bought it for you."

A beat passed. "Yeah, but I didn't want him to give me so much money."

It looked like he and Morley settled on real estate as the reason. "So, how much did your son contribute?"

"I don't remember. It was a lot."

An egret who'd been standing so still that it looked like a garden ornament took two steps toward the lake. "I'd remember someone giving me a large sum of money."

Porter silently shrugged.

"Especially since it wasn't that long ago."

"You got a better memory than me."

"Did you ever pay Mr. Morley back?"

"Not yet. But he said it's okay."

"Who do you think killed Coby and Martin?"

"I don't know. Maybe Vape; he comes every day to see his mother. He's into the mercy killing thing."

"It's not mercy killing if there's no suffering."

"I don't know about that stuff."

"We can subpoena the records and find out how much your son gave you for the condo."

"He gave me most of it. But you know, I needed more, for, you know, furniture and stuff."

"And as a friend, Morley wanted to help you and gave it to you?"

"Yep."

"He's a good friend to have."

"Yes, sir."

"Since you're friends, when was the last time you went out, socially, with Mr. Morley?"

"You know, I can't remember."

"When's the last time you went to his house?"

"I don't think I ever went there."

"You have him over to your place?"

He shook his head.

"He helped you buy the condo and you never had him over?"

Another shrug. "Mr. Morley is busy."

"I'd think he'd make time for his friends, especially those good enough to give money to."

DR. BILOTTI WALKED into my office while I was on the phone and settled into the chair in front of my desk. I finished my call and said, "Hey, Doc, sorry. I forgot to call you back."

"That's okay. Is everything all right?"

"Not bad."

"How is Mary Ann?"

"She's actually doing pretty good. No more attacks, and swimming twice a day seems to help."

"That's good news. Physical exercise is an important component to maintaining a normal lifestyle."

"We're walking every night as well. And eating super clean."

"Excellent."

"That's because you don't have to eat it. She stopped drinking wine too. It's up to me to finish the bottle."

"You know, a little red wine may help, but no more than a glass every now and then."

"Really?"

"Some studies indicate that resveratrol may help with inflammation, but there's nothing conclusive. A glass of vino every couple of days with dinner isn't going to hurt her."

"She'll want to bounce it off her neurologist."

"Of course. I'm glad she's doing well. And how are you doing?"

"This case is driving me crazy."

"I meant you. How are you doing?"

"Me? I'm okay, really. Things are settling down. You know, the shock just threw me for a loop. As long as it stays like this and I know it's going to get a bit worse, we'll be okay."

"It may require an adjustment or two, but you'll handle them. Just take it a day at a time and keep things in perspective; it'll work out just fine."

"You're right."

"What's the status of the Palm Shores case?"

"Like I mentioned, the suspects we have either work there or have visited every day for years. The apartments were sanitized before a new occupant moved in, and there wasn't forensic evidence on the bodies exhumed."

"Ah, just like the good old days. Check for fingerprints, use a little intuition, and wait for a slipup."

"I'll take the forensics train anytime. Without it, it feels like we're never going to solve this."

"But you like to say that eventually a mistake is made?"

"They know we're looking at them."

"You're the mind man. You told me more than once that psychopaths can't help themselves, and it's true. They're irrational and unpredictable the majority of the time. Sooner or later, they'll screw up."

Bilotti was right. I appreciated the reminder.

50

Mary Ann came out of the bedroom in a bathing suit. "Can you wait a half hour to eat? I want to take a swim before dinner."

"Sure. You didn't get in the pool today?"

"Of course I did. In fact, I hit a new record this afternoon."

"You did?"

"Yep. Sixty-two laps."

"You're turning into a real fish."

"I want to get up to a hundred."

"Don't overdo it."

"I'm going to do whatever it takes to beat this."

"That's my girl."

"And if I can't beat it, I'll slow this damn thing down to a crawl."

"Come here."

I wrapped my arms around her and said, "Save a little energy for later. This bikini is making me horny."

Coming in the kitchen, my phone vibrated. I didn't recognize the number and swiped the call away. "Did you see that homework? Why are they learning about China? Why isn't she being taught American history? Geez, nobody is going to know what this country was founded on."

"Take it easy, Frank. They hop back and forth during a particular time period."

"They do?"

"Yep."

My phone vibrated again. "Just wanted to be sure."

"Who keeps calling?"

"The number doesn't ring a bell. Probably a robocall."

"They don't call back to back."

She was right. I dug my phone out and checked the number. Like magic, it started vibrating.

"Who is this?"

In the hushed tone of an undertaker, Vuvich said, "Galena. She is worried about Vape. He is up to no good."

"What are you talking about?"

"He is being strange."

"How is that?"

"Galena watch him. He go into hallway, check the worker's schedule on bulletin board. Then he go into nurse office when she not there. Vape always leave after dinner, but he still here, moving like tiger. Galena ask why he still here, he say mother is sick—"

"He's concerned about her."

"But the night Mr. Coby died, she was sick that night too, and Martin too."

"Mrs. Vape was sick on both nights the murders occurred?"

"Yes, Galena remember because he stay, after Galena leave."

"Keep an eye on him until I get there."

"Galena have to leave; other lady needs me to do the bathing."

"Can you wait a few more minutes? I'll be there in twenty minutes."

"Galena wait and watch."

"Good, don't say a word to anyone about this. Act normally. I'm leaving now."

Mary Ann said, "You're going out?"

"Yeah, I'm sorry, but there's a chance the killer is going to strike again."

"Oh my God. Who is it?"

"Brian Vape. He's into some twisted version of euthanasia." I headed to the garage. "Say good night to Jessie for me."

I TURNED off the siren but kept the lights on until reaching Tin City. Surveying the lot, I pulled into a visitor spot next to the only car in the row. Vape's Prius was nowhere in sight. I didn't consider myself a religious person, but I found myself praying that he hadn't escaped after striking.

The receptionist started to greet me, but I put a finger to my lips. A TV was blaring somewhere. I whispered, "I don't want to announce I'm here. Don't tell anyone, or it will be considered obstruction of justice."

"Uh, okay, okay."

"Do you know where Galena Vuvich is?"

"She said to tell you she was in Miss Ringer's apartment, it's one twenty-four."

"What about Mrs. Vape's apartment?"

"Uh, one thirty-one. A couple of doors down, on the other side, opposite the door for the stairs."

The gathering space was nearly empty, just one lady watching a black-and-white movie on a huge TV. I quickened my pace, entering the resident's wing. Passing a dozen doors, I quietly knocked on Ringer's door.

The door opened a few inches, revealing a security door chain. Peering up at me was Galena. She unlatched the lock. I stepped in.

"Everything okay?"

"Yes."

"Did you see anything?"

She shook her head. "Galena open door every five minutes to see, but nothing."

"Is Vape in his mother's place?"

"Galena think so."

"Would he think it was unusual for you to ask how his mother was?"

"No, Galena worry about all residents."

"Okay, I need you to do something before you leave. I need to know if he's still here."

She nodded.

"Knock on their door; tell him you're about to leave and wanted to make sure his mother was all right."

"Okay."

"But keep it short; say nothing else. If he wants to talk, tell him you have to go."

She went into the bedroom to tell her client she'd be right back. Keeping the door open a crack, I watched her totter to the apartment. It took Vape a minute to answer.

Vuvich shook her head. He must have invited her in. They chatted for a moment and she came back.

"What did he say?"

"His mother still sick, and he was worried about her."

"That's all?"

"Yes."

"Good. You can leave now."

She nodded. "Galena must let Miss Martha know."

Maybe everyone in the Ukraine referred to themselves in the third person, but I couldn't get used to it. "I'm going to take up a position somewhere and keep an eye on him. Give me a minute or two before you leave."

Slipping out of the apartment, I surveyed the corridor. The stairwell across from the Vape apartment seemed ideal for a stakeout. There was a map of the footprint of each floor by the reception area. Not having memorized it, I went to check if there was a better location.

One look at the map confirmed the stairwell as a prime position to monitor Vape. From the looks of it, his mother's apartment had a porch, but I wasn't sure there was access to the outside.

Debating whether to ask the receptionist, Galena breezed by me, waving on the way out. The back of the apartment Vape was in faced a grassy area on the left side of the main building. I went into the great room. The woman watching TV had dozed off. I wished I could sleep with the volume she had it on.

A large seating area shaped like half a hexagon jutted out of the rear of the room. I went to the windows and looked at the rear of the wing where Vape was. The porches were screened in completely. No way for him to escape from the back.

Leaving the room, I heard the woman ask me to find the remote. She wanted to raise the volume further. I found it stuck between the cushions of a blue couch, handed it off, and left.

I turned into the hallway. Vape's head was sticking out the door, looking in the opposite direction. I retreated then snuck a look. Vape stepped out, crossed the hallway, opened the door to the stairway, and disappeared.

<h1 style="text-align:center">51</h1>

Discounting a call for backup, I ran down the carpeted hallway. I opened the stairwell door slowly, hearing the door on the next floor slam shut. I took the stairs two at a time to a landing.

Peering through the door's window, I saw Vape look left before heading right. He disappeared around a corner. Stepping out of the stairwell, I followed him.

Sticking my head around a corner, I caught Vape putting his hand on a doorknob. He stepped into an apartment. I took off after him. He wasn't going to kill anybody on my watch.

A step before reaching the apartment, I drew my weapon. Vape was shouting. I heard another male voice. Was an elderly resident fighting back?

I burst in. "Police! Put your hands up!"

The room was empty.

To my left I heard a woman moaning. In a doorway two pairs of legs were intertwined on the carpet. Leading with my gun, I rushed into the room.

My jaw dropped.

Vape was pinning Ryan Hall to the floor. A woman, in bed, was slumped over sobbing.

I trained my gun on the men. "On your stomachs. Now! Both of you!"

I swiveled my head. "It's okay, ma'am. Everything is going to be all right."

Straddling Vape, I cuffed him as he said, "The woman needs help. He drugged her."

"What did you give her?"

Glassy eyed, Ryan said, "I didn't do anything; it was him."

"That's bullshit. You—"

"Shut up! Both of you!"

Climbing onto Ryan, I cuffed him as well and patted both men down. They were clean of weapons but had articles in their pockets.

I pulled my phone out and called the station dispatcher. "This is Detective Luca. We have a possible overdose on a female in her eighties. She's unresponsive. Get a medic unit and ambulance rolling to Palm Shores. It's off Forty-One in East Naples. Send a couple of cars as well. I have two under arrest."

"Got it. Is she conscious?"

"Barely."

"Do you know what drug was involved?"

"It might be Rohypnol."

"An ambulance is on the way. The paramedic unit should have Romazicon; it's an antidote. If there's oxygen where you are, get her some, it'll counter an impaired respiratory rate."

"Will do. Tell them to hurry; she's out."

Grabbing the phone off the nightstand, I called the receptionist about the oxygen. I tried to awaken the woman, but she was out cold. It took all my restraint not to put a slug of lead into both men.

As a siren wailed in the distance, I approached Vape and Ryan.

"Get up." I helped lift them onto their feet. As I put on latex gloves, I read them their rights. It was time to search both men more closely, starting with Ryan.

I dug out two sets of keys and an auto fob from one of the front pockets of his jeans. In the other, three one-dollar bills. I bagged them along with his wallet and cell phone.

As I ran my hands to Ryan's ankles, I saw a hypodermic needle just under the bed.

"What do we have here?"

Vape said, "That's what he used."

Ryan said, "No way, man. It's yours."

"Shut up!"

Using my phone, I took several pictures of it. Then I took a pen out, rolling the syringe out with it. I carefully placed it into an evidence bag.

As I began reaching into Vape's dungarees, he said, "You got this all wrong. I was trying to stop him."

"Save it. You'll have your chance to talk later."

"But I didn't do anything. Mrs. Bilock will tell you."

One front pocket had keys and a Listerine packet. The other had a handful of bills and a thumb drive. I put them in an evidence bag with his wallet and phone. We'd do a thorough search at the station.

Pushing both men into the bathroom, I said, "The two of you better hope she recovers."

Strobe lights leaked through the window as a pair of aides and the receptionist came into the room rolling an oxygen tank.

The aides hooked her up, and I told the receptionist to go

back and direct the paramedics. Then I instructed the aides, "One of you stay with her. The other one, make sure no one comes in here."

I watched the aide firmly pat the woman's hand. There was no response. She was dying a slow-motion death. As a pair of paramedics rushed into the room rolling a gurney, I said, "I think she's been poisoned with roofies."

"We got it. We'll stabilize her and get her over to NCH downtown."

On the phone, one checked her vitals, relaying the information to a doctor. He nodded to his coworker, who prepared to stick her with a needle. I hoped like hell they'd arrived in time.

I asked the aide to get me the details on the woman's family and to inform them their loved one was being taken to the hospital.

Two uniformed officers marched in. I gave them the rundown and told one to bring Vape and Hall in and the other to secure the crime scene.

As my suspects were being escorted out of the bathroom, the paramedics lifted the woman onto the gurney.

"Is she going to be okay?"

"We'll see."

"But you gave her that shot, didn't you?"

"Yeah, but there's no guarantee, especially at her age."

The hallway was jammed with terrified residents. I waded through, telling them Mrs. Bilock was going to be fine and to return to their apartments.

As if Hitchcock were directing, it started raining when I stepped outside. I called Derrick.

"What's going on?"

"You're not going to believe it, but it looks like Vape and Hall were in it together."

"The Palm Shores homicides?"

"Yep. I just caught both of them giving an overdose to a female resident."

"Jesus! I don't get it. Hall with Vape? It doesn't fit, unless Hall is into euthanasia, which would be weird since he works for a senior living outfit."

I hopped into the Cherokee. "Maybe it's not euthanasia. Hall makes money by filling apartments."

"So why work with Vape?"

"I don't know yet, but I caught them red-handed with this poor lady. I hope she pulls through."

"She in bad shape?"

"Touch and go. The paramedics said because of her age they don't know if she'll make it or not."

"Damn it."

I put the wipers on and pulled onto Tamiami Trail. "I'm heading in. I'll see you later."

At the Goodlette Frank light, I called Mary Ann to let her know it was going to be a late night. A very late one.

Vape and Ryan were still being processed. I couldn't avoid the paperwork, but I didn't need or want to be around for the strip searches. Tucking a file under my arm, I headed back to my office.

Derrick was looking over the evidence bags laid out on my desk. "Morley called twice already. You think he's involved with them?"

"Not sure at this point. But it's altogether possible. Vape would be a natural ally for Morley. Vape kills on some twisted principle, and Morley profits from it. Maybe he contributes to his cause or something."

I fingered the bag containing the thumb drive I'd taken off Vape.

"I'm curious as hell about what's on this."

"Shouldn't the lab guys be dealing with that?"

"We'll just take a peek. It'll help with the interview. Get another bag ready for when we're done."

I pulled on gloves, broke the seal and pulled it out. I slid the top open. "Look at this. The entire time, I thought it was a thumb drive."

Double stacked, six round pills sat in the belly of the tube. The white tabs were all marked with the name of the pharmaceutical company Roche and the number one in a small circle.

"Let's see what Dr. Google says this is." I typed Rohypnol into the search bar and navigated to images. The second line of photos had three tabs that matched perfectly. It was the date-rape drug.

"No surprise."

"They're legit pills."

"Vape's a doctor. He probably wrote his own script. Pretty damn convenient, for a killer."

"This is unbelievable."

"Bag it back up."

I fingered the bag with the keys we'd taken from Ryan Hall. "Am I missing any possible connection with Porter?"

"Porter? I don't see it. It would have to be one convoluted conspiracy."

"We can't discount it, but I agree it's unlikely. We need to determine if any of these keys are masters for Palm Shores. I don't trust Morley to answer truthfully. Maybe Porter can compare them to his."

"I'll call him and send over pictures."

I picked up the phone and made a quick call. Hanging up, I said, "Bastards."

"What's the matter?"

"The lady's in ICU."

"Damn shame."

"I'm going to get a couple of search warrants going before talking to these punks."

V APE 'S HANDS were cuffed in front of him. Usually I'd take them off to help soften someone up. The problem for me was that the image of the woman fighting for her life had burned into my head.

Yanking a chair out, I plopped onto it. I flicked the video camera on and recited the formalities, including his right to an attorney.

"You understand you are entitled to the presence of counsel."

"Yes, I don't need one."

"This is your chance to talk. Tell me what you were doing in Mrs. Bilock's apartment."

"I was trying to save her. Hall was going to kill her."

"Start at the beginning."

"I was in my mother's apartment. She wasn't feeling well after dinner, so I hung around to keep an eye on her. We were watching TV when I heard what sounded like someone coming into the apartment. I shouted and went to see what was going on. I opened the door. Hall was going into the stairway, and I followed him."

"What made you do that?"

"I don't know. Earlier I had seen him, and he was high as a kite, acting weird. I don't know, maybe in the back of my head I thought he was going to hurt someone or himself."

Hall had been glassy eyed. "Then what?"

"I followed him up the stairs. He got out and was like hugging the wall, going down the hall. It was weird. Then he stops in front of a door. I knew it was Mrs. Bilock's. She talks to my mother all the time. He had keys in his hand. He opened the door and went in. It didn't make sense at that hour going in like that, so I went after him."

"Hall opened the door with a key?"

"Yes."

"How many keys on the ring?"

"I don't know. I was down the corridor."

"You go in the apartment, then what?"

"I went in kind of slow. No one was in the living room, so I went to the bedroom, and that's when I saw him doing it."

"Doing what?"

"Giving her an injection. He had done it already. I knew it was going to kill her, so I attacked him."

"You're a doctor: weren't you concerned about getting stuck with the needle?"

"I didn't think. I just went crazy. It was surreal, happening so fast I didn't have time to think."

"Then what?"

"I got him on the floor, and you came in."

"That's quite a story."

"It's not a story; that's what happened."

"I think you and Hall were in it together."

"No, that's crazy. I was trying to stop him."

"You're a hero, then."

"Anybody would've done what I did."

"And you had nothing to do with it or with Hall?"

"I swear. I would never do something like that. He's sick."

"But you're an advocate for euthanasia."

"Come on, that was no mercy killing. It was murder."

"Speaking of murders. You were here, late, during the time when Mr. Coby and Mr. Martin were killed."

"It's possible. My mother gets sick often. She's in her eighties."

"Convenient excuse."

"She's in her eighties and gets sick often. That's not convenient. It's the reality of aging."

"You understand my skepticism. Your mother happens to

be sick, giving you cover to be here when each of the attacks took place."

"What can I tell you? The fact is, she didn't feel well. She's sick with a bad cold right now. You can check with her doctor on the other dates."

We would check on that, but he could have chosen to act only when he had an excuse for being there late. And even if he were telling the truth, the picture he painted still didn't hang straight. "You know, I could almost believe your story except for one fact."

"What are you talking about? What fact?"

"Every victim was given Rohypnol." I paused before saying, "The same drug in your pocket when you were arrested."

The color drained from his face. "I can explain."

53

———

Derrick had been watching the interview. After ending it, we conferred in an empty interrogation room two doors away from where Ryan Hall was stewing.

"You buy what he said about the roofies?"

"He believes in euthanasia, but I don't know if I buy carrying around pills to commit suicide in case he's badly injured or incapacitated."

"He's fairly young, but his father got cancer around his age."

I'd also gotten cancer at a young age. "There's time with stuff like that. I'm wondering if he keeps it around to give it to his mother if she takes a dive."

"Hm, that makes more sense."

"Call the lab, no, go down there. In addition to lifting prints off the needle, ask them to shave a piece off one of the pills Vape was carrying. Have them dissolve it; see if it turns blue. If so, we may not have to wait for the spectrometry test to see if they're from the same batch."

Derricks shoulders sagged. "That's a shortcut I should have thought of."

"I got the idea from you. Oh, and check to make sure the pills Vape had amount to a lethal dose for someone like him."

"You got it."

"Good, while you hit the lab, I'll see what Hall has to say for himself."

Looking through the window, Hall was fidgety and looked like shit. How I thought he looked like Seacrest was beyond me. I wasn't better than most eyewitnesses.

As soon as I entered the room, Hall put his game face on and said, "How is Mrs. Bilock?"

"Critical, thanks to you."

"It wasn't me; it was Vape. He—"

"Hold on." I switched the recording device on and recited the formalities, including his right to a lawyer. Hall declined. It was funny. Most people thought being interviewed without a lawyer was a sign they were innocent. We knew that and never took that into consideration.

"What were you doing in Mrs. Bilock's apartment?"

"I was checking on her."

"Why?"

"I was making my rounds. You know, since Mr. Coby and Mr. Martin, residents were scared. So I've been walking the complex a lot of nights. It reassures them everything is going to be all right."

"You were patrolling the hallways?"

"Yes." He smiled. "It's no joke, but don't forget, if it happens again, I won't be able to get anyone to move in here."

It was the second time he didn't call the murders what they were. "What made you go into her apartment?"

"I heard something. It sounded like she was asking for help, and the door was open."

"It was open?"

He squirmed in his seat. "Yes, Vape left it open."

That didn't line up. When I followed Vape in, Hall was already inside. "You're in the apartment, then what?"

"He was giving her a needle. It stunned me, you know."

"What did you do then?"

"I jumped him right before you came in."

"So, Vape was in the apartment, giving Mrs. Bilock an injection?"

"Yeah, like I said, I couldn't believe it."

"That doesn't fit. I saw Vape enter the apartment and followed him in. You sure about the order?"

Scratching his forearm, Hall said, "Maybe you're right, you know; the whole thing is jumbled up. Yeah, he was there, then I came in and saw what he was doing."

Some suspects never confess. Some deny until they don't. Then it's like a light goes on and they talk nonstop. You can't ask a question to clarify because you're worried they'll stop talking. Others give it up bit by bit: I wasn't there morphs into I was, but I didn't do anything. Then it was the other guy did it. You go over it a thousand times and admissions leak out.

Hall may be the latter type, telling the truth on some kind of layaway plan. He was a drug user and was used to lying. I was almost certain he was involved. The question was whether he was working with Vape or Morley.

We needed to search Vape's home and Hall's apartment. There was a high probability we'd find something to sharpen who the killer or killers were.

54

———

Vape had weathered two days in the county jail better than most. He shuffled into the room in an orange jumpsuit. He nodded at me. His attorney, Michael O'Brien, pulled a chair out for him and said, "I'd consider it a professional courtesy if you'd uncuff my client."

I took them off his wrists, leaving the leg shackles intact. Recorders on and formalities recited, I began, "Mrs. Bilock is still in critical condition. It's high time you took responsibilities for your actions."

"My client has repeatedly denied any involvement in this heinous crime. He was trying to stop an attack."

"We conducted a search of your home, Mr. Vape, and found an interesting array of material promoting euthanasia of the elderly."

"You're completely misinterpreting the material."

"Really?" I lifted a page up and read, "Living with Killing; It's Not Your Fault; You're Helping Not Hurting; along with several books on the dangers of overpopulation. It's damn grim reading."

O'Brien said, "Possession of written materials representing a wide range of viewpoints is not a crime."

"That's correct, Counselor, but I'm sure the DA would like a jury to know what we found during a search."

"I'm innocent. My belief in mercy killing to relieve suffering has nothing to do with this."

"You were in possession of a deadly dose of the same drug injected into Mrs. Bilock and used to kill two others. Why would you carry those around?"

O'Brien said, "My client is a physician. The medicines were obtained legally via a prescription."

"Yes, one he wrote himself. Why? Saying you had them in case you became incapacitated is something I'll never believe."

Vape leaned toward his attorney and whispered in his ear. O'Brien said, "I advise against it, but if you feel strongly, go ahead."

"I don't know anything about you, but if you witnessed the pain and suffering that my father had to endure, you might feel differently. I kept the pills in case my mother found herself in a situation like that. She begged me to put her out of her misery if it happened to her, and I agreed. You can ask her. She'll back me up."

That admission made more sense, giving him a good excuse to be in possession of a deadly dose.

It was time to feed a bit of bullshit to entice Vape to open up. "Mr. Hall has confessed to his role in the murders, saying you worked together."

"He's lying. I hardly ever spoke to him."

"You want to answer that again? I've seen you and Hall chatting on several occasions. You looked like childhood friends."

"Detective Luca, if you have evidence to prove my client's involvement, I suggest you share it."

"With all due respect, Counselor, your client was in the room at the time the attack occurred. As you may know, yours truly arrested him there. The DA is comfortable holding Mr. Vape based upon the evidence we have at this time."

"We have the right to know what evidence you have."

"It won't be long, Counselor."

There was a chance that a partial print found on the barrel of the needle was Vape's. We were waiting for an expert from the FBI's Fort Myers office to weigh in. The print on the plunger was Hall's.

If Vape and Hall were working together, a possible theory had Vape, a doctor with access to drugs, preparing the needle and Hall delivering the deadly dose.

DARK CIRCLES under Hall's arms turned his jumpsuit two tones of orange. Sitting next to him was Lawrence Nestle, the attorney known as Mr. Plea. He wasn't considered expensive and could stay that way because he'd rarely go to trial.

I hoped to quickly determine if the source of Hall's perspiration was drug withdrawal or the advice about a plea.

Striding into the room, I said, "Good afternoon, gentle-men. Is there anything I should know before we begin?"

Hall picked at a cuticle and Nestle said, "Nothing at the moment. You may proceed."

Recording device activated, I stated the time, date, and attendees, then asked, "You and Brian Vape were in Mrs. Bilock's apartment. Were the two of you working together?"

"I had nothing to do with it. He was the one trying to hurt her."

"Then explain why your fingerprint, a thumb one at that, was on the needle's plunger."

"How would I know? Maybe it got there when we were fighting."

"You said the door to the apartment was open."

"That's right."

"I think you gained access with the master key you were carrying when you were arrested."

Nestle said, "My client is the salesperson for Palm Shores. He possesses the master key to all the apartments there. Showing apartments is an integral part of his responsibilities."

"I followed Mr. Vape into the apartment. You were already inside. We believe it was Mr. Vape who was trying to prevent you from murdering again."

"That's bullshit."

Nestle whispered in his ear and Hall scowled.

"In a search of your apartment, we found drug paraphernalia, including a crack pipe."

"It's not mine."

"Your fingerprints are all over them."

"My friend left his stuff in a bad place, so I moved them."

"We're getting DNA off it. I'm sure it will be yours."

"I can do what I want in my house."

"Smoking crack is illegal, even in the privacy of your own home."

"So, I was doing a little partying. It's no big deal."

"What happened with your Bentley?"

"I didn't want it anymore."

"According to the dealer, it was repossessed. You hadn't made a lease payment in nine months."

"The car had all kinds of problems. They wouldn't fix them, so screw them."

"Le Mer is a fancy place to live. And expensive."

He shrugged.

"You're five months behind on your rent."

"I don't see the relevancy of private transactions that my client has entered into."

"They're relevant, Counselor. It is our belief that your client is addicted to crack cocaine. And that Mr. Hall's addiction created a desire for money so great that he took part in a scheme to kill residents, knowing that he'd earn commissions from the residents who'd replace them. The only question in my mind is whether he acted alone or with a conspirator."

Hall said, "You're crazy, you know that?"

Two quick knocks on the door sounded before it swung open. Derrick stuck his head in, saying, "May I have a quick word?"

I excused myself and stepped into the corridor. "What's going on?"

"The lab confirmed that the pills Vape had on him came from a different batch than what was in the needle. And we only found evidence of one script that Vape wrote, and all the pills are accounted for."

"Vape was telling the truth. He was trying to stop Hall."

"Looks that way. Should I cut him loose?"

"No, not yet. Hold him. I'm not convinced Hall acted alone."

Stepping back in, I resumed questioning Hall.

"I want to ask you about a twenty-thousand-dollar payment you received from Fred Morley. Why did he give you so much money?"

"He owed it to me."

"For what?"

"None of your business."

"It certainly is my business. I believe the payment was a bonus to sweeten the incentive to kill."

"I had nothing to do with anything."

"Fred Morley is your boss, right?"

"You know he is."

"I hear he's a very tough man, very domineering, like a bully."

"He's not—"

Nestle put his hand on Hall's forearm. "May we have a few moments of privacy?"

"Absolutely, Counselor." I got up and said, "Let me take those cuffs off."

55

CLICKING THE RECORDER OFF, I STEPPED OUTSIDE THE ROOM. Hall was close to talking. Nestle was going to advise him to throw Morley under the bus and cut a deal. I went right to the one-way mirror.

Hall was shaking his head no. Nestle put a palm up and looked directly at his client, putting one finger up, then a second, and finally a third. It looked like he was making sure Hall knew he was in deep trouble.

Hall started speaking, but Nestle shook his head and spoke, patting him on the hand. Hall nodded. The slimmest of smiles flashed across Nestle's face. Unwilling to give Hall a chance to change his mind, I knocked on the door and entered.

I flipped the recording switch on and resumed the interview.

"We were speaking of Mr. Morley."

"Detective, my client possesses information we believe the sheriff's office would be interested in."

"What kind of information?"

"Concerning the primary conspirator."

"I'm all ears."

"He's willing to divulge all he knows, but we're looking for an acknowledgment of the importance of what he knows."

"We're always willing to consider cooperative efforts as long as someone confesses."

"We understand the need to make admissions, but we're looking for something more concrete in nature for consideration."

"If you can give us Fred Morley, we'll show our appreciation by recommending as much leniency that sentencing guidelines permit."

"As far as Mr. Hall serving any time, our preference would be he serve it at the Gulf Correctional Institute. Can we have an assurance our request would be considered?"

"As you know, Counselor, we can't guarantee that, but we'll present it to the judge."

Nestle turned to Hall and said, "Answer the detective's questions."

"Did you conspire with Fred Morley to murder residents of Palm Shore?"

"Yes."

"Whose idea was it?"

"His, he told me to do it."

"How did that come about?"

"He knew I needed money, and he gave it to me on the condition I'd do it."

"Are you referring to the twenty-thousand-dollar check that Fred Morley wrote to you three months ago?"

"Yeah, that one and a couple of others."

"Which others?"

"I don't remember exactly."

"The checks were from him?"

"Yes."

"Do you recall what bank they were drafted on?"

"No."

I asked the question that was haunting me and held my breath, "Did you, Fred Morley, or anyone else murder any residents of Water's Edge or any other facility?"

"I didn't."

"What about anyone else, like Fred Morley or Ben Porter?"

"They could've. I know he gave money to Porter."

"Was that to entice him to kill a resident?"

"What else could it be for?"

"Let's go back to the beginning. You said Fred Morley approached you, offering money if you did as he asked and you killed certain residents. Where did this conversation take place?"

"In his office. He called me in."

"When was this?"

"I don't remember the day."

"With a conversation like that, I'm sure you'd remember something, the time of year, maybe it was around a holiday."

"Yeah, now I remember, it was a couple of days before Christmas."

"He came to you about killing someone just before last Christmas?"

"Yep, it was crazy."

"Whose idea was it to use a drug like Rohypnol?"

"His."

"Where did he get it from?"

"I don't know. Why so many damn questions. I told you he did it."

"We need to establish how the crime was conceived and executed. Why don't we take a ten-minute break? Would you like something to eat?"

"Yeah, a Coke and some candy."

I grabbed his treats and asked Derrick to arrest Morley. It was going to be one of the longer days in my career, but once it was over I'd have plenty of time to spend where I belonged, with my family.

MORLEY HAD his elbows on the table. His attorney hadn't arrived yet. I entered the interrogation room.

"This is a huge mistake, Detective Luca. I'm going to sue the county for wrongful arrest."

"That's your prerogative, but we have enough to hold you."

"Exactly what?"

"Your coconspirator, Ryan Hall."

He slumped in his chair. "What did he tell you? That I was involved?"

"Yes."

"Look, I love the kid like a son, but he has a disease; it's called addiction. I tried to help him as best as I could. After all I've done for him, I can't believe he'd turn on me. I want to know what he said."

"You want to talk without an attorney present?"

"Absolutely."

I pulled a chair out, turned the recording device on and had him waive his right to counsel.

"Ryan Hall claims the two of you were working together and that you enticed him with money to kill."

"That's ridiculous. He's a desperate young man with serious problems. The idea I'd collaborate with him is simply crazy."

"You gave him twenty thousand dollars."

"That's because he promised to use it for rehab."

"Why didn't you tell me that when I asked about it?"

"I didn't want to embarrass him. And by the way, the money I lent to Ben Porter was for a lawyer for his grandson. The kid had a DWI and didn't want his father to know."

"Why didn't you pay the rehab facility directly?"

"I wanted to, but he said I didn't trust him, and well, it was stupid, he never went in. I tried so hard to help him. He promised he'd go. I guess I wanted to believe him."

"Isn't it true that you kept him employed, not because he was a good salesperson, but to enrich yourself by having him kill residents that had made down payments."

"That's outrageous. I should have fired him, but I was afraid he'd get worse. That's what did in my son. Without the structure of the job, he went down like a rocket."

"Your son?"

He nodded. "My son Andrew, he overdosed ten years ago. He battled addiction since he was twenty but went into rehab and cleaned himself up. We were proud of him. He was doing good, living and working in Atlanta for Delta. He got mixed up in it again but seemed to be making progress when he was fired for being high on the job. It was all downhill from there. He went on some kind of binge and died less than two weeks later."

"I'm sorry to hear that."

"I didn't want it to happen to Ryan."

It was disturbing to see the pain he was in, but I had to wall off my emotions. It was time to drill down on Morley as much as I could before his mouthpiece showed up.

56

I WAS ALMOST 100 PERCENT POSITIVE WHO WAS TELLING THE truth, but since the Barrow case, that was never good enough.

It was unconventional and probably breached protocol, but I had the feeling my idea would work. I put the cuffs on Hall and sent a text to Derrick. As soon as he answered, I got up and led Hall out of the room.

Hall stopped short when he saw Derrick and Morley heading our way. Morley's face broke into a smile.

"How are you doing, Ryan?"

Ryan stared at his shoes. "Okay, I guess."

"It's going to be all right. You start taking care of yourself, and everything else will work out."

Ryan's shoulders began to heave. "I'm sorry. I didn't mean to . . ."

"It's okay. We straightened everything out. The important thing is for you to get treatment. You do that, and everybody is going to be fine."

Ryan was sobbing. I grabbed him under an armpit to prevent him from collapsing.

Morley said, "Don't get upset. I'm there for you. I'll see you as soon as possible. Okay?"

Ryan nodded, and I led him to a holding cell. He was going to be behind bars for a long time. Lucky for him, Mrs. Bilock pulled through, but killing two and attempting another would earn him a serious sentence, no matter his drug addiction.

He'd get dried out, but for how long was the question. Drugs were nearly as easy to get in jail as they were on the street. If he could keep clean, he'd have his chance with the parole board in fifteen years.

Morley was a better man than I'd given him credit for. There probably was no answer to whether the way he handled Hall and his drug addiction made things worse or better. I felt for him and hoped he wouldn't carry any guilt over it.

THE SUNDAY PAPER may not be as thick as it had been when I was growing up, but it was still stuffed with items I had no interest in. Flipping through the sections, I pulled out the advertisements and real estate section.

A picture of a house on a sidebar caught my attention. It was the Longboat Drive home that had been burglarized. It was a new listing. It looked like the Crenshaws had been shamed into moving out of Naples. We wouldn't miss them, I thought as I sipped my coffee.

Jessie stuck her head out the slider. "Daddy, can we go see the baby now?"

"In a little while; it's too early to go. Don't you want to see her when she's awake?"

"How long till we go?"

"After breakfast. Mommy will take her swim and then we'll go. Okay?"

"I'm going to swim with Mommy." She took off. I put the paper down as I contemplated the excitement Derrick was feeling. It was impossible to beat the buzz you received greeting your child as it came into the world.

It only felt like a year ago when we were blessed with Jessie. She was six now. I did the math. In eight years or so, she'd be babysitting for Derrick's daughter. I saw our families growing closer.

Mary Ann came out in her bathing suit. She still looked good in a bikini, and more importantly, was doing well in her battle with MS. Goggles in hand, Jessie was right behind her and jumped into the pool. I still got nervous when she'd disappear underwater.

I watched Mary Ann ease into the water and got back to my paper. On the third page was an article on a piece of legislation before the Florida senate. The nursing home and assisted living industries were fighting a bill that would require changes in how deaths were handled.

It was disgusting that it took two deaths at Palm Shores to force the politicians to act. It wasn't what I thought should be done, but it was better than the way it was presently being handled. According to the piece, it looked like the bill would pass, and if so, Governor DeSantis said he would sign it into law.

Like they say, some good comes out of every bad situation.

The next book in this series is, Dangerous Revenge. Find it in eBook & Paperback.

I hope you enjoyed reading this book as much as I enjoyed writing it. If you did, I'd appreciate it if you would write a quick review on Amazon or your favorite book site. Reviews are an author's best friend and even a quick line or two is helpful. Thanks, Dan

OTHER BOOKS BY DAN

THE LUCA MYSTERY SERIES

Am I the Killer

Vanished

The Serenity Murder

Third Chances

A Cold, Hard Case

Cop or Killer?

Silencing Salter

A Killer Missteps

Uncertain Stakes

The Grandpa Killer

Dangerous Revenge

Where Are They

Buried at the Lake

The Preserve Killer

No One is Safe

SUSPENSEFUL SECRETS

Cory's Dilemma

Cory's Flight

Cory's Shift

OTHER WORKS BY DAN PETROSINI

The Final Enemy

Complicit Witness

Push Back

Ambition Cliff

You can keep abreast of my writing and have access to books that are free of discounting by joining my newsletter. It normally is out once a month and also contains notes on self- esteem, motivational pieces and wine articles.

It's free. See bottom of my website: www.danpetrosini.com

ABOUT THE AUTHOR

Dan is a USA Today and Amazon best-selling author who wrote his first story at the age of ten and enjoys telling a story or joke.

Dan gets his story ideas by exploring the question; What if?

In almost every situation he finds himself in, Dan explores what if this or that happened? What if this person died or did something unusual or illegal?

Dan's non-stop mind spin provides him with plenty of material to weave into interesting stories.

A fan of books and films that have twists and are difficult to predict, Dan crafts his stories to prevent readers from guessing correctly. He writes every day, forcing the words out when necessary and has written over twenty-five novels to date.

It's not a matter of wanting to write, Dan simply has to.

Dan passionately believes people can realize their dreams if they focus and act, and he encourages just that.

His favorite saying is – "The price of discipline is always less than the cost of regret"

Dan reminds people to get the negativity out of their lives. He believes it is contagious and advises people to steer clear of negative people. He knows having a true, positive mind set makes it feel like life is rigged in your favor. When he gets off base, he tells himself, 'You can't have a good day with a bad attitude.'

Married with two daughters and a needy Maltese, Dan lives in Southwest Florida. A New York native, Dan has taught at local colleges, writes novels, and plays tenor saxophone in several jazz bands. He also drinks way too much wine and never, ever takes himself too seriously.

He puts out a twice-a-month newsletter featuring articles, his writing and special deals and steals.

Sign up at www.danpetrosini.com